FANTASY IN LINGERIE

Lingerie #6

PENELOPE SKY

Contents

1. Vanessa   1
2. Bones   17
3. Vanessa   41
4. Bones   67
5. Vanessa   109
6. Bones   147
7. Vanessa   157
8. Bones   201
9. Vanessa   217

Thank you!   245
Also by Penelope Sky   247

1

Vanessa

I sat at the easel in Bones's place and stared at the blank canvas. I struggled to decide what to paint. My artistic inspiration seemed to have disappeared from my body. After that conversation with Bones in my kitchen, I felt dead inside.

The fight within me disappeared.

I felt hopeless, like there was nothing I could do to control my own destiny.

Bones really did own me.

I took that gun from my father, thinking Bones wouldn't suspect it. I wrapped it up in a sweater in my bag, assuming Bones wouldn't look through my things. But he was a trained assassin, so of course, he predicted exactly what I would do.

How could I fight my way out of this?

I laid my cards on the table, and he knew I didn't have a decent hand. Now he knew I didn't want to kill him, and when it came down to the final moment, I didn't have the strength to pull the trigger.

But he didn't kill me either.

Maybe we were in the same boat.

But he seemed intent on killing my family, and the only thing stopping him was me. As long as I continued to be the woman in his bed, he would leave my family alone. It was the only defense I had to protect my family. By pleasing him, my parents were safe every single night when they went to sleep.

It was a small sacrifice to make.

But what happened when Bones got bored with me and found another woman who caught his attention?

I'd be screwed then.

When my brush didn't touch the paint or the canvas, I knew I was wasting my time. I had no motivation to create something. The last piece I'd made was hauntingly beautiful, and it seemed to suck all of my energy away.

I finally gave up and set my tools aside.

I didn't want to be there anymore.

I just wanted to be alone, to clear my head and think things through.

I walked down the hallway and found Bones sitting at his desk in his office. He had a map in front of him, along with a silver pistol. He held a blade in his hand, and he was spinning it around his fingertips as he considered the map in front of him.

I tapped my knuckles against the doorframe before I walked in.

He kept circling the blade around his fingertips as his gaze lifted up to mine. A glass of scotch was on the desk, and he was shirtless despite the winter temperatures outside the window. Black ink covered him everywhere, only leaving patches of tanned skin in certain areas. No one in my family had tattoos and I'd never been interested in getting one myself, but when I looked at his beautiful body covered in art, I found it appealing.

It made his hard body look even better.

I stopped at the desk and stared down at what he was looking at. Three spots on the map had been circled with red ink. It was a map of Milan, and the three different points were about two miles apart each.

He watched me, his face etched in lines of annoyance.

I crossed my arms over my chest, wearing the white smock that had splashes of paint on it. My hair was pulled back and out of my face. "What are you working on?"

"My next victim." He stabbed the knife into the desk, making the blade stand up and the hilt point toward the ceiling.

When I looked at his desk closely, I saw all the marks where he'd stabbed the knife before. "Who is it?"

"The man who killed my mother."

My eyes turned back to him, the information unexpected. "You know who did it?"

"Max figured it out."

"Who's Max?"

"One of my boys."

"So…what now?"

"I'm figuring out a plan. He's not an easy target. He's the leader of a group called the Tyrants. They deal with illegal trafficking of weapons and such. They aren't big by any means, not like the mob. But it won't be easy. He doesn't go many places alone, unless he's fucking a whore, of course."

"Sounds dangerous."

"Always is." His hands came together, and he stared at me with his icy blue eyes.

"Do you think it's worth the risk?"

"Meaning?" he asked.

"You're putting your neck on the line, but your mother is gone."

He obviously didn't like that response because his eyes narrowed. "And if it were your mother?"

I'd do everything I could to avenge her. But I didn't voice that answer out loud, not when he already knew what I would say. "This guy sounds dangerous. Be careful."

"Maybe he'll kill me and solve your problem."

Since I couldn't solve the problem on my own. The idea of Bones being killed while trying to find justice for his mother made me sad, not happy. I should want him dead, but even in that context, I didn't want him to die. "I don't want you to die trying to avenge your mother. I hope you prevail and get the justice she deserves. Your family deserves peace."

His narrowed eyes slowly softened, just a little.

"But I hope I have the strength to kill you before you lay a hand on my family. Because I don't want to have to avenge them the way you have to avenge your mother."

The softness disappeared, and his gaze hardened once more. "Is there something you needed?" His tone was cold, as frosty as his eyes.

"I'm going back to my apartment. I can't concentrate, so I'm just wasting my time."

His reaction didn't change, but he didn't seem happy with that answer either. "Why can't you concentrate?"

It was a stupid question because he already knew the answer. "I just want to be alone for a while."

"To do what?"

"Get away from you." I told him the honest truth, getting to the point because I wasn't afraid to tell him how I felt. With every passing day, I hated him more than I had before. But I hated myself the most. The gun hadn't been loaded, but even if the reality had been different, I was too stupid to squeeze the trigger.

I was a disgrace.

He didn't react at all, like those words meant nothing to him.

I turned around without waiting for a response and walked out. I grabbed my bag from the bedroom then stepped into the elevator.

He didn't come after me.

HE LEFT me alone like I asked.

When I was in my apartment, I got some work done and then went out with some friends. We went to dinner and then to a bar. I drank a lot more than I usually did. A few guys hit on me, but I didn't show any interest.

Every man didn't compare to Bones.

I hated that he was right.

I wasn't attracted to a single man in any place we went. Even the hot ones weren't hot enough. They weren't built the way Bones was. They weren't dark the way he was. They didn't possess the right kind of confidence, the right kind of intensity. He was all man, all power. And he really did make all the others look like boys.

Little boys.

This man had ruined my life. I wasn't the same person anymore. My tastes had changed, and now I was attached to a man who didn't give a damn about me. He was my worst nightmare but also my wet dream.

Ugh, I hated him even more.

I walked home because I was so warm from drinking and being inside those stuffy clubs. I was just in my black dress and heels, the cold air feeling so good against my skin. I'd probably catch a cold by the time I returned to my apartment, but I didn't care.

I didn't care about anything anymore.

Bones isolated me from the world, preventing me from telling anyone what was really going on. He kept me in a cage with no bars, trapping me in my own mind. He made me obedient by giving me the best sex of my life.

It was a fucked-up situation.

A dark car pulled over to the curb, and the passenger window was down. Some guy had his arm hanging out, and he grinned at me in the creepiest way. "Hey, you want a ride?"

"If I wanted a ride, I would get a taxi." I focused my eyes forward and kept walking. "Now, fuck off."

The car kept driving next to the curb, moving slowly and matching my pace. "Ooh…she's got a mouth on her."

"If you like my mouth, you should meet my foot."

"Sure," he said. "I'd love to meet anything on that gorgeous body."

I rolled my eyes. "Leave me alone. You're creepy and gross."

"Gross? Come on, baby. Get to know me first."

Baby. I hated hearing him call me that. Only one man called me that, and only one man was allowed to. I'd tried to stop him from using the term a few times, but I eventually gave up because it started to feel right.

Now it felt so right that hearing another man say it felt innately wrong. "I don't want to get to know you. Now drive away before I rip your balls off and bury them in the snow."

"Why don't you lick my balls instead?"

That was it. I slipped off my heel, marched over to the window, and slammed my shoe right into his face, hitting him hard. "I told you to fuck off."

"Ah, shit!" He leaned away and covered his nose because it was bleeding. The heel of my shoe hit him good.

I slipped my shoe back on and kept walking. "That's what I thought."

"Bitch." The car came to a stop, and three men got out and came toward me.

I was drunk and stupid, so of course, I wasn't afraid. "You wanna go, assholes? Bring it." I dropped my clutch and brought my hands to my chest, tightening them both into fists. "I'll castrate every single one of you."

All three halted before they came near me, unanimously scared of me. They glanced at each other then slowly stepped back, not turning their backs on me.

"That's right. Get the hell out of here."

They ran back to the car, jumped in, and peeled out. They sped down the street like they were being chased by the police. I could hear the engine working hard even when they were out of sight. "Pussies…" I picked up my clutch before I turned to keep walking and slammed right into a brick wall.

I bounced back, almost losing my balance.

He grabbed me by the elbow and righted me, jerking me back until I slammed into his chest again.

Bones.

He looked down into my face, more pissed than I'd ever seen him. He grabbed me by the neck and squeezed, cutting off my air supply slightly just to make his point. His fingers shook because he wanted to squeeze me harder, but he found the strength to resist.

Now, it all made sense.

The men weren't running from me.

They were running from him.

"You're better than this." He squeezed me a little harder, the vein in his forehead throbbing. The cords in his neck were thicker than they'd ever been before. He was in a black hoodie with jeans, most of his ink covered, with the exception of a few lines popping out of his neckline and sleeves. "You're too fucking smart for this bullshit. What the fuck are you thinking?"

"I'm not thinking…" I'm too drunk and depressed. I'm stuck with a man I hate, waiting around for him to finally butcher me. I'm too pathetic to retaliate because I've become so damn attached to him. "I can't even go out to a bar and pick up a guy because I don't want anyone but you. I can't even kill you if I had the opportunity because I don't want to. So I'm fucking stuck in this torture. Maybe I don't care about walking home in the dark because there's nothing to care about. Whether I survive tonight or not, I'm dead anyway." I pushed his hand off my neck then shoved him hard in the chest, but instead of moving him, I shoved myself backward and toward the concrete.

He caught me and lifted me into his arms. He carried me down the sidewalk in the direction of my apartment, which was just a few blocks away. My heels were left behind, and my clutch was stuffed in his waistband.

I hated him for rescuing me, but the second his powerful arms were around me, I wanted him again. I wrapped my arms around his neck and buried my face in his skin, clinging to his warmth. I was suddenly cold now that the anger had passed, now that the adrenaline wasn't pumping in my veins.

He must have known I was cold before he set me on my feet. He pulled his sweater over his head and then yanked it down over my body.

The warm cotton immediately surrounded me, keeping me warm and enveloped in his smell. It reached my knees, and the sleeves were far too long for my short arms. It was like a blanket instead of a piece of clothing.

He lifted me into his arms again and carried me the rest of the way.

"How did you know where I was?"

"Your tracker."

"Were you watching me this whole time?"

"I'm always watching you, baby. Anytime I'm not with you, I know exactly where you are."

It made me feel safe, but it also made me feel powerless.

"I'm disappointed in you."

"I'm disappointed in myself..."

"The woman I know wouldn't give up. She wouldn't put herself in a dangerous situation like that. She wouldn't be so fucking stupid."

I rested my face against his chest and closed my eyes, not wanting to listen to his anger anymore. "Stop..."

"I'm never going to stop, baby. I'm fucking pissed at you right now."

"It's not like you care about me anyway..."

He said nothing to that and carried me the rest of the way home. He pulled a key out of his pocket and let us inside.

I'd never given him a key. "Where did you get that?"

"The landlord."

"Why would he give you a key?"

"Because he wanted to live." He locked the door behind him then carried me to bed. He lay me on the sheets then pulled off the sweatshirt and unzipped the back of my dress before he yanked it off my body. It smelled like booze, cigarettes, and cheap perfume. He grabbed my thong and yanked that off too.

I lay there, drunk and somber.

He undressed next then got into bed with me. He

spooned me from behind and wrapped his arm around my waist. His face pressed into the back of my neck, and his breaths fell across my skin. Despite how hard he was, he didn't make a move to fuck me.

It was anticlimactic. "What are you doing?" I asked into the darkness.

"Sleeping. Now shut up."

"You never just sleep."

"Shh. You're a lot more annoying when you're drunk."

"And you're a lot more annoying when you aren't fucking me. That's all you're good for. So why aren't you doing it now?" I turned over to look at him.

He stared at me furiously. "Did it cross your mind that maybe I don't want you right now? Because I don't like stupid women who do stupid shit? I've never found you less attractive than I do right now."

I slapped him across the face. "Fuck you."

He turned with the hit and clenched his jaw, but he didn't hit me back.

"I went out tonight looking to get laid. That's what I want."

"Really?" he countered. "Because it looked like you were trying to get raped."

I smacked him even harder this time, hitting him so hard my palm left a print.

He took the hit again without striking back. "Shut up and go to sleep."

"Shut up and leave."

"Do you want me to fuck you or leave?" he countered. "Pick one."

I kicked him under the sheets. "I want you to leave and never come back. I wish my family killed your mother so you'd never been born. That's what I want, asshole."

I knew I'd crossed a line when he gave me that look, that look that told me I may not live long enough to take my next breath. His eyes narrowed with hostility, and there was so much threat in that expression I was actually scared.

Scared that this would be the moment I died.

His chest rose and fell rapidly as he breathed through his anger. He reminded me of a tiger about to rip his prey to shreds. He had the muscle to pull off each of my limbs. He could even tear off my head if he wanted to.

But what would he do first?

I scooted away, becoming more afraid as the seconds passed. I couldn't move as quickly as I wanted to because I was too drunk to think straight. I was just confused...scared and confused.

He left the bed, yanked on his clothes, and then stormed out.

The door slammed behind him.

And then it was quiet.

I lay back on the pillow, the room spinning a little because I'd had way too much to drink. I wasn't even sure how I walked in a straight line on the sidewalk.

Once Bones was gone, the bed felt ice-cold. I started to feel scared, scared that I was alone in the apartment without him there. What if those men came back for me? The paranoia started to kick in, my illogical thoughts taking over.

Bones saved me. If he hadn't been there at that moment, I might be sitting in the back of that car. Or I might be naked in some strange bed, being raped by three different men. I put myself in a dangerous situation, and he saved me.

My father would be so disappointed in me.

I started to lose my grip on reality, this psychological prison taking its toll.

I hated myself.

I hated myself for being so weak.

This wasn't me.

I wasn't Vanessa Barsetti anymore.

Now, I couldn't sleep. I stared at the ceiling, feeling a little bit of the warmth that lingered after he left. I was naked under the sheets, and I wished his naked skin was pressed against mine. I missed the man I hated. I only felt safe when my tormentor was with me. It was a paradox, but it didn't change the way I felt.

I wished he would come back.

And then I heard the sound of the front door. It was quiet, opening and closing softly.

Was it him?

Or was it someone else?

I sat up in bed, trying to understand if I'd really

heard the sound or not. I could just be paranoid, hearing things that my mind invented.

Then he stepped into the room, his shirt already gone and his jeans coming undone.

Thank god.

I moved to my knees and reached for him, needing that strong body on top of mine. I needed his warmth to feel safe, needed to be underneath him to know that nothing could hurt me.

He got his jeans off then moved to me. "I'm here, baby."

My arms circled his neck, and I kissed him, kissed him with passion. I kissed him in apology, touching his body everywhere to make up for the way I'd savagely struck him. I fell back and pulled him with me. "Don't leave…"

"I won't." He separated my thighs with his knees and moved inside me. "I'm staying right here with you."

"Don't ever leave me." I pulled on his hips and felt his big dick all the way inside me. I moaned when I felt him, finally feeling safe now that this strong man was on top of me, inside me.

"I won't."

"Promise me." I kissed him hard on the mouth, feeling him so thick and deep.

His hand fisted my hair, and he deepened the angle, giving me more of his cock. He breathed into my mouth and gave me slow and deep thrusts. "I promise."

2

Bones

I could tell she didn't remember much from the night before.

She woke up at noon, threw up in the bathroom, had a glass of water, and then swallowed a few painkillers to thwart her migraine. She got back into bed, crawling like she could barely stand. She lay on the sheets, her eyes closed.

I went into the kitchen and made lunch. I made her a sandwich with chips and a few cookies. She didn't have a kitchen table, so I set everything on the coffee table. I walked back into the bedroom and found her exactly as I left her. "Baby."

"Hmm?" She didn't open her eyes.

"You should eat. I made lunch."

"Lunch?" she whispered.

"Yes."

"What time is it, then?"

"Almost one."

She sighed and dragged her hands down her face. "I feel like shit."

"You should." I wouldn't sweep her behavior under the rug like it was acceptable. She was stupid and reckless, and if I hadn't promised I wouldn't tie her up, she would be chained to the bed on her stomach so I could slap her ass with a belt. "Now, get up."

She finally sat up, still naked because that she hadn't put any clothes on.

I grabbed one of my shirts and helped her get it on. Then I grabbed a fresh pair of panties from the drawer and pulled them up her long legs.

Her face was pale and she looked ill, but she still looked like the beautiful woman who stole my fascination. Once she was covered in my shirt, she was even more beautiful. She ran her fingers through her hair and pulled it out of her face. Then she blinked a few times as she woke up.

I watched her, making sure she didn't fall over. "Come on."

She finally got out of bed and walked into the living room. She sat down on the floor in front of the food and started to eat slowly, her eyes squinting because the afternoon light strained her eyes and her migraine.

I shut the curtains.

She instantly looked better.

I sat on the other couch and watched her, hating myself for what was happening. I'd stormed out of the apartment because she'd insulted me in a brutal way, but I walked back in because I didn't want to leave her.

I also didn't want to leave her when she was that drunk.

If someone else came into the apartment, she wouldn't be able to defend herself.

Leaving her unprotected made me sick to my stomach, so I walked back inside.

And I knew she wanted me to come back, even though she'd asked me to leave. I was hard before I made it through the door. She lay there, wishing I was between her legs and on top of her. She acted like she didn't need me, but there was no place in the world safer than by my side—or underneath me.

I found her exactly as I'd predicted, yanking me back into the bed.

And making me promise never to leave again.

She never wanted me to leave.

I didn't want to leave either.

But I didn't know what kind of promise I'd made—I just knew I wanted to keep it.

Now I stared at her from the other couch, taking care of her because she was weak like a newborn deer that couldn't walk. I'd never cared for another person in all my life, but now I was cooking for her and making sure she didn't throw up and choke on her own vomit. I was making sure she had enough fluids and she was making it to the bathroom okay.

How did I get here?

She only ate half of her food, but that was plenty. At least she had something in her stomach. She started to lighten up a bit, the migraine finally disappearing and the color coming into her cheeks.

I kept staring at her.

She finally met my look.

Minutes passed. The staring continued.

I wondered how much she remembered. I wondered if she remembered the desperate way she pulled me back to bed and begged me to stay. I wondered if she remembered how good the sex was, how we kept going for an hour straight even though she was exhausted. I wondered if she remembered the promise she asked me to make.

She ran her fingers through her hair and sighed.

The second she was coherent, I had a few things to say. But I waited until the right moment.

"I'm sorry." Her apology rang through the air and filled the silence. It lowered the tension between us, addressed the obvious issue that needed to be dealt with. "I just… It was stupid."

"It was really fucking stupid."

"Does it sound like I'm disagreeing?"

"But I don't think you understand just how fucking stupid you were. Walking down the street in nothing but a dress and heels when it's thirtysomething degrees outside—"

"I know."

"Provoking those assholes like you're invincible—"

"I know."

"Interrupt me one more time and see what happens." My nostrils flared because she was pissing me the fuck off. I had something to say, and it was a lot more valuable than the excuses she was going to give.

She crossed her arms over her chest, her mouth shut.

"The Vanessa Barsetti I know is strong, smart, and doesn't take shit from anybody. She's not reckless and arrogant. This pathetic, lifeless version of you is insulting to you and everyone who knows you. Don't give up like that ever again. Don't have a damn pity party for yourself and expect people to care. Stand on your two feet and fight. You hate me for putting you in this situation? Then find a way out. Don't walk down the street at one in the morning dressed like that and think rape and death are a solution. My mother ended up in a dumpster. You want the same fate?"

She held my gaze, the remorse in her eyes. "I'm sorry for what I said—"

"I don't want your apology. I know you meant what you said." I know she wished I were dead so she would be free. She couldn't kill me herself, so she needed someone else to do the dirty work.

"But I didn't mean what I said… Your mother was innocent. She was just involved with a cruel man. It's not any different than our situation…" She turned her gaze to the ground. "I didn't mean it, and I immediately felt terrible after I said it."

I believed her. "Don't ever pull a stunt like this again."

"I won't," she whispered.

"Promise me."

She turned back to me, the look in her eyes telling me she remembered what she'd said last night, the promise she'd asked me to make. A slight look of embarrassment flushed over her cheeks, and she quickly hid it. "I promise."

HER LEGS STRADDLED MY HIPS, and she rocked her body back onto my length, taking my long cock as far as she could go before she moved up again. Her hands gripped my biceps for balance, and her tits shook with the thrusts.

I stared up at her, my hands on her hips as I guided her up and down. I watched her breathe through her exertion, drops of sweat collecting on her chest and the back of her neck. There was nothing sexier than watching a woman like her fuck me. I knew she was trying to make up for what she'd said to me, and fucking my cock was the best way to do that.

I had no complaints.

I felt her cream coat my length, pressing all the way down my shaft and to the base of my dick. She was always so wet for me, and tonight, she seemed even wetter than usual. I didn't press my feet against the mattress and thrust up with her.

I wanted her to do all the work herself.

She angled her face close to mine and kissed me, arching her back deeper so she could keep taking my length all the way to the hilt.

Fuck, I loved her kisses. I loved her pussy. I loved everything about her. I could do this forever…come inside this pussy over and over.

Her lips trembled against mine, and her breathing began to change. Her nipples got hard, and her pussy started to squeeze me.

I'd made her come enough times to know when she was about to explode.

"Come for me, baby." I gripped her harder and pulled her onto my length at a quicker pace. "Come all over my dick."

Those words pushed her over the edge, and she came all around me, squeezing me like an iron fist. She moaned against my mouth, her back arching and her hips working harder to take my length. She screamed in my face, panting until she finished.

I propped myself up on one arm and fisted my hands into her hair. I knew I was about to fill that pussy with all my seed, stuff it with my arousal. Coming was the best part of sex, but the entire act, from beginning to end, was my favorite when it came to her. Sex had never been this good, this passionate.

"Give it to me," she said against my mouth. "I want it."

"You want my come, baby?"

"Please."

Jesus. I gripped the back of her neck and came, pumping mounds of come inside that wet slit where it belonged. I already felt like a man with my above-average height and six-percent body fat, but coming inside this woman made me feel like a king.

She moaned when she felt me throb inside her, taking all the come she'd just asked for. She took it deep, doing her best to accommodate my entire size so she wouldn't spill a drop of my precious come.

My hand dug into her hair and I kissed her hard, devouring her lips with mine. My fingers felt her sweat, and I loved knowing she gave herself a workout just to please me.

She spoke against my lips. "Thank you…"

"That was all you." I just lay there and enjoyed it, enjoyed this beautiful woman riding my dick.

"No…thank you for saving me." She rested her forehead against mine, her eyes on my lips. "All you did was stand there and scare them away. I don't think I could have fought them off…not when I was that drunk. So if you weren't there——"

"Shut up." I didn't want to hear her talk about that night and what could have happened. If someone took her and forced themselves inside her, I would have lost my mind. I would have tortured every guy before I killed them—and then killed their entire families for further punishment.

This was my woman. No one touched my woman unless she wanted to be touched.

She pulled back and looked at me, her eyes narrowed in annoyance at my cold words.

"I don't want to talk about that night ever again. I will always be there to protect you, but do me a favor and don't give me a reason to save you. Be smart, be safe."

Her eyes dropped their hostility, and she rubbed her nose against mine. "I will."

I SAT in my office while Vanessa worked down the hall in her studio. She'd been there since we'd gotten back from her place about an hour ago.

The elevator beeped when someone tried to rise to the floor.

Only a few people had the code to get into the lot. One of them was Max. But no one had the new code to the elevator except me.

I walked into the living room and hit the button to see the person through the camera.

It was Max, standing there in a black leather jacket with a full beard and a bag hanging on his shoulder. "What?"

He glared into the camera. "Fuck you, Bones. Let

me in."

"Let's meet somewhere, then."

"Why?" he countered. "I'm here. And what we're gonna talk about can't be discussed in public."

Which meant we were talking about Joe Pedretti. I hit the button and allowed him inside the elevator.

"Asshole…" He stepped inside and disappeared from the camera.

The elevator rose, and he walked into my living room less than two minutes later. He greeted me with a nod then stepped farther into the room. "Thanks for the warm welcome."

"A heads-up would have been nice."

"You got three whores up here again like last time?" He grinned, loving the angry look on my face.

I hoped Vanessa didn't hear that, not that I should care how she would feel about it. "No."

"So your off-limits woman is here." He sat on the couch, his satchel still hanging over his shoulder.

I didn't answer him, not wanting to confirm or deny it. I grabbed a bottle of scotch from the cabinet along with two glasses. I sat on the other couch and filled the glasses before I slid one toward him. "What's up?"

Now that the liquor was poured and we were seated, Max turned serious. "Still going after Joe?"

"Fuck yes."

"Have you really thought about it? I'm telling you, it's not a good idea."

"Even if I die in the attempt, I'm still doing it." My

mother risked her life to take care of me, and I wouldn't be a man if I didn't honor that. She'd spread her legs and let men assault her so I had a place to live and food in my stomach.

Max shook his head slightly. "I still think it's stupid. I'm telling you this as a friend, not a business partner. You're risking everything you've attained. She's gone, man. You can't bring her back."

"Doesn't matter."

He sighed then rubbed the back of his neck. "You know I have your back forever…but I can't be involved in this. I'm not risking my life for something that doesn't make sense. It would be different if she were still alive—"

"I never asked for your help."

"So you're going to track him down and kill him all by yourself?" he asked incredulously.

"Yes."

"He's surrounded at all times."

"I'll figure out a way."

"And if you don't kill him and he comes after you, you'll be hunted for the rest of your life. Do you understand that?"

"This is a blood war, Max. It continues until there's no more blood." I drowned myself in a sip of scotch, needing it to take the edge off.

"What about this Barsetti woman?"

"What about her?"

"Isn't she worth sticking around for?"

I didn't want to talk about her, especially when she could be listening down the hall. "Enough, Max. Nothing you say is going to change my mind. So just drop it. Give me the intel you have, and let's move on."

He stared at me, his brown eyes filled with disappointment.

I ignored his look, ignored his stress. We'd been friends for decades, had done business together for a long time. If I died, it would hit him hard. If I had kids, he would be their godfather. That was how tight we were.

Footsteps sounded down the hallway, and Vanessa appeared in black jeans with a purple top. Her hair and makeup were done, and clearly, she decided to take a break from her work at the worst time.

Max eyed her appreciatively, looking at her from head to toe. "She's really not worth sticking around for?"

"Shut up or I'll stab you."

Max grinned but kept his eyes on her. "Hello, sweetheart."

"It's Vanessa." Only I called her by another name.

Max's eyes turned back to me, and his smile faltered and was replaced with something else, a meaningful look.

"Hi." Vanessa stopped at the back of the couch, standing right behind me. "I didn't know we were having company."

"Neither did I," I said coldly.

Vanessa's hands moved to my shoulders, where her thumbs pressed into my hard muscles. She gave me affection in public, and something about that turned me on. She claimed herself as mine, showed Max I was her man without me having to ask her to. "I'm Vanessa."

The corner of his mouth raised in a smile. "Max. Nice to meet you."

I enjoyed the feeling of her fingers pressing into the cords of my muscles. Felt so good, so deep. I'd never let anyone touch me like that. I didn't even let a woman massage me. But I liked the way Vanessa touched me.

"Bones talks about you a lot…and now I can see why."

My threatening gaze turned back to him. "Shut up before I break your jaw."

He ignored me. "Has he told you about this idiotic plan to kill Joe Pedretti?"

"Yes," she whispered. "He mentioned it."

"Well, you should convince him not to go," he said. "Because it's a stupid idea, and it's going to get him killed."

"She wants me dead," I said bluntly. "So you won't hear her talk me out of it."

Her hands paused against my shoulders, and after a few seconds, she started to rub me again.

Max eyed her for a moment before he turned back to me. "Doesn't seem like it. So, shall we get to work?"

I pushed her hands off my shoulders even though I

wanted her to keep touching me. "Baby, go back to painting. Max and I have stuff to take care of."

She walked around the couch and into the sitting area. "What if I don't want to paint?" She challenged me, her vicious attitude back in full force. "I can go wherever I want to go. And this is where I want to be."

I tried not to smile.

She sat on the other couch and crossed her legs. "I might learn something."

I held her gaze before I turned back to Max. "What have you got?"

"I know he's going to be at the opera on Saturday." Max pulled out the folder and pushed it toward me. "He's got three men on him at all times, including one driver. They're always armed and wear bulletproof vests. From what I can tell, he doesn't experience too many attacks, but he's certainly prepared for them. If you hit him during the opera, you can slip something into his drink or stab him in the crowded room."

"He might not know it was me."

"That's the point."

"I don't want anyone else to know it's me. But I want him to look me in the eye before I kill him."

Max sighed. "That's not going to happen, not unless you kidnap him. The man is never alone. My guy watched him for three days straight. This guy is accompanied at all times. Maybe you could do a drive-by and take out his men along with him, but even then, it's not exactly what you want."

No, it wasn't. This was personal, so it couldn't be done with a simple bullet between the eyes.

Vanessa listened to Max before she turned her gaze on me. "Doesn't he like to kill prostitutes?"

I couldn't keep the sarcasm out of my voice. "Yes... that's why we're sitting here."

Her eyes flared in annoyance. "Does he still like to kill prostitutes?"

"As far as I know," Max said. "Why?"

"What if you got him alone with a hooker?" she asked. "He can't have men watching him then, right? Unless he's into that..."

The thought hadn't crossed my mind, and I felt stupid for not thinking of it. I turned to Max.

He was already looking at me. "That's not a bad idea. We could have a woman take him to a motel. You could be there waiting for him."

"I'd have to get the woman out to make sure she's not a witness. Otherwise, she could rat me out."

"True," Max said. "And you'd want to get her out of harm's way."

"Yeah," I said. "She would have to get him in the room, get out, and then let me finish him. And she'd have to keep her mouth shut. But even if we pay her off, his men could hunt her down and torture the information out of her. She would be easy to find if she found work on the street."

"I have an idea," Vanessa said.

"Yeah?" Max said. "What is it, sweetheart?"

"Call her that again, and I'll turn you into a punching bag," I threatened.

Max grinned. "Someone is pussy-drunk…"

Vanessa watched the anger on my face, watched the way I became possessive of her even with my closest friend.

"I told you she was off-limits," I said quietly. "I meant it."

Max raised both hands in the air. "Alright. Loud and clear." He turned to Vanessa. "You've got him under your thumb. Make sure you use that against him if you can."

She was under my thumb just as much.

"What's your idea?" Max repeated.

Her gaze turned to me, like she knew I wouldn't like the idea before she even announced it. "I could be the hooker."

I stared at her, dumbfounded.

Max didn't expect the idea either.

"I could be at the right place at the right time, and I could take him to the hotel. I would leave and let you do what you need to do. They'll never find me again because I'm not really a prostitute. And I'd wear a wig."

"And he definitely wouldn't pass up the opportunity to grab her," Max said. "She fits his type perfectly."

I was still staring at Vanessa, shocked by the offer she'd just put on the table. Why would she help me? Why would she put herself in danger when she got nothing out of it? "What do you want in return?"

She took a deep breath before she answered. "My family. I do this for you, and you leave them alone."

Max sat between us, eyeing us back and forth. He stayed quiet, knowing he had nothing to do with this.

"No." I wasn't giving up my revenge just to fulfill a different vendetta.

"You could use me," Vanessa said. "I could make this work."

There was no doubt in my mind that she could. If I put her in play, he would be just as obsessed with her as I was. "I'm not putting you in danger like that. I'll find another way."

"It's too risky to have someone else do it," she said. "You know that."

"I'm not sparing your family," I repeated.

She crossed her arms over her chest, her eyes shifting back and forth as she considered it. "Bones—"

"No." I wouldn't change my mind. I wouldn't drop my vendetta, and I wouldn't put her in danger. Joe would take one look at her and eye-fuck her to death. He would imagine the ways he would fuck her before he killed her. He would fantasize about leaving her in a dumpster somewhere.

Not my woman.

"Okay…" Vanessa said. "Then I'll do it anyway."

Max looked up again and shifted his gaze to my face.

"What?" I asked blankly.

"I'll lure him anyway—to help you." She stared at

me with those beautiful green eyes, those thick lashes making her feminine and beautiful. "I want you to kill him, Bones. I know this is important to you. I know you'll never stop until you get justice for your mother. So let me help you."

My eyes were wide open as I stared at her, unable to believe she'd offered to put herself in a dangerous situation just to help me. She got nothing out of it, but she wanted to see me succeed. "No. I don't want another man looking at you. I don't want him touching you. I don't want him anywhere near you." The idea of Vanessa ending up in a dumpster like my mother made me sick to my stomach. If someone was going to kill her, it was going to be me—no one else. "You aren't involved in this. End of story."

I DIDN'T COME out of my office until later that night. My stomach was full of scotch and I was at the perfect level of drunkenness, so I wasn't as angry as I usually was. Vanessa made that offer to help me, but I was ticked she'd made the gesture at all.

She was mine.

I wasn't going to let my enemy think, even for a second, that he was going to fuck my woman.

When I walked into the living room, she was sitting on the couch in one of my t-shirts and her panties. This was normal now, a habit to see her in my t-shirts on a regular basis. The shapeless cotton was somehow sexier than the lingerie I got her. Knowing it was my clothes she wanted on her back turned me on.

She must like my smell.

She turned her eyes away from the TV and met my gaze. "Still mad at me?"

"I'm always mad at you." I stood behind the other couch, my hands gripping the back.

"Yeah…I picked up on that."

I gripped the furniture tightly, my knuckles turning white. I wasn't livid with her for the comment, but livid that I found her so painfully beautiful in my clothes. I should demand her to take it off and never wear it again, but I didn't. I didn't because I loved the way it looked on her—so fucking perfect.

"I'm sorry I offered. I was just trying to help you."

"And why the fuck would you try to help me?" I hissed.

"You saved me just a few nights ago. I don't consider that ancient history."

I looked away, not wanting to see the gratitude in her eyes. "I didn't save you because I care. I saved you because you're mine. Your pussy is mine, and your life is mine too. So don't be grateful."

"I am anyway. You know one of my biggest fears is to be raped…I fear that more than death."

I listened to her beautiful voice, the strength mixed with the vulnerability.

"I thought you would want to use your prisoner to

achieve your goals. If I die in the process, what does it matter to you?"

"Because I want to be the one who kills you, not my enemy." I turned back to her, seeing the stoic expression on her face. I thought a statement like that would hurt her, but she seemed to be immune to it at this point. "And I don't want him looking at you or touching you."

She sighed quietly. "I agree with Max. I think this is a bad idea, and you're going to wind up dead."

"Wouldn't that make you happy?"

"No, it wouldn't," she said seriously. "I want you to avenge your mother. Then I want to be the one who kills you—or my family. I guess we both feel the same way about each other's deaths…we want them to be done the right way."

"But only one of us is going to survive. Who do you think it'll be?"

She looked so small on my couch, her long legs tucked toward her body and her dark skin so soft and beautiful. She made herself at home, like a pet that kept me company. A more beautiful woman had never been here, had never sat on that couch and looked at me like that. "Honestly, I think we're both going to die at the end of this. Who goes first…I'm not sure."

I listened to her say it so pragmatically, and that made me respect her. Death was a part of life, and there was no getting around it. The best thing to do was to accept it with dignity, to greet death as an old friend. "I think you're right."

"You'll kill me first. But my family will make you suffer for it."

"You have so little faith in yourself?" I questioned. "You don't think you could do it?"

She looked away. "I've obviously proven that I can't do it…"

So did I. I could have killed her two months ago, but she was still here. She was still breathing. She was still in my bed every night, taking my dick and my come. She was the only woman I'd had by my side for this long. She was the only one who managed to keep me entertained, keep me interested. The sooner I killed her, the sooner I'd have my revenge against the Barsettis.

But the idea hadn't crossed my mind.

I kept telling myself I would kill her.

But was I lying to myself?

"So…three whores at once?" She gave me a look full of accusation—and disappointment.

So she had been listening. I didn't deny it, having no shame in what I'd done. "Yes." I held her gaze, not backing down and not making apologies.

"I'm surprised you pay for sex. You don't seem like a man who needs to."

"I don't—but I like it."

Now her look changed, the anger coming through.

"I like sex as a transaction. It's fun—and then it's over."

"After what your mother went through, I'm surprised you would resort to that."

"That's exactly why I do it. I treat them well, and they have a good time."

She turned away, her eyes brimming with suppressed rage.

"Jealous?"

"No," she spat. "I'm just afraid you've given me something."

"I'm clean."

"Are you sure?"

"A hundred percent."

But she still looked angry, still pissed off.

That's how I knew I was right. "You are jealous."

"I'm really not."

I couldn't stop myself from grinning. "Is it because they were whores? Because I've been with a lot of women. If that makes you jealous—"

"It's because there were three of them…at once."

I tried not to gloat, but that was nearly impossible. "And why does that bother you? Being with three women isn't much different from one."

She sighed through her teeth. "Shut up."

I grinned wider. "This is killing you."

She finally got off the couch and stormed down the hallway toward the bedroom. "'Night."

"Baby." I followed her, enjoying this way much more than I should. She was afraid I would kill her and her family, but she was actually jealous of me being with other women. She was jealous the way I was jealous, the way I got angry when I imagined her in a bar while men stared at her. I watched her tracker that night because I didn't want her to go home with anyone else. If she did…I didn't know what I was going to do.

I followed her into the bedroom and saw her pull down the sheets.

She ignored me, pretending I wasn't there.

I leaned against the doorframe and crossed my arms over my chest. "Baby."

"Just shut up, Bones. I'm going to sleep." She turned off the bedside lamp.

I walked around the bed until I was standing over her. "I'm not going to lie…I'm really enjoying this."

"Yeah, I can tell." She turned over and faced the other way.

I leaned over her and pressed kisses to the shell of her ear. I breathed into her canal before I spoke. "I'm a very jealous man when it comes to you…and I've never been that way before."

I could feel her relax underneath me, those words meaning something to her.

I waited for her to turn back to me, to give me her full gaze.

"They were before you."

"And has there been anyone after me…?" She hated herself for asking the question. I could feel it.

I kissed her ear again. "You know the answer to that, baby."

"I want to hear you say it."

I kissed her neck and her jawline. "Only you." I grabbed her chin and turned her gaze on me. "Alright?"

"Alright," she whispered.

"I was staring at your tracker that night because I was worried you would go home with some other guy. And if you did…I was probably going to kill him."

Her fingers wrapped around my wrist as I held on to her chin. "There's no one I wanted to go home with…"

"I know. I know you only want me."

Shame flooded her gaze.

"And I only want you," I whispered. I'd never said that to a woman before. I'd never been monogamous my entire life. I hadn't even been with one woman for more than a few days. But I'd been fucking Vanessa for a couple months, and I felt like we were just getting started.

"Then it's just you and me?" she whispered. "Until this is over…?" Her hands moved underneath my shirt and felt the muscles of my body.

We didn't have a lot of time together, and I didn't want to spend that time in between another woman's legs. I only wanted to be with her, and I certainly didn't want to share her. "Yes. Until this is over."

3

Vanessa

Sapphire texted me. *Let's have dinner tonight.*

Does Conway know about this? When it came to living with Sapphire, he didn't want me around much. When I stayed with him for a few weeks, he couldn't wait until the day I left.

Yes. He hasn't seen you since Christmas, and he misses you.

I laughed out loud because that was bullshit. *Nice try, Sapphire.*

Conway and I are in Milan working at the studio. It's going to be a late night so we thought we would grab dinner afterward. Are you free?

My whole life revolved around painting and Bones, so I was free all the time. *Yeah. When?*

How about an hour?

Alright.

We'll pick you up.

I was staying at Bones's place, and by the time I got

ready and headed over there, I might not make it in time. *I'll just meet you there.*

You know how Conway is. He'd rather pick you up.

My brother's protective bullshit wouldn't work right now. I didn't want him to be aggressive when this monster watched every little move I made. Conway would be caught off guard and be powerless. He had a little one on the way, and the last thing I wanted was for him to get hurt. *Well, I'm not home, so I'll just meet you there.*

Where are you?

I really hated the nosiness of my family sometimes. *I'm out with some friends. I'll just meet you there, alright?*

I did not need their suspicion right now. If Conway figured out Bones was involved in my life, the blood war would start, I'd be dead, and everything would go downhill from there.

I went to my closet in the bedroom and pulled out an outfit to wear. It was freezing outside, so I decided on jeans, boots, and a nice sweater, and my thick jacket and scarf.

Bones walked inside, dressed in his running shorts and t-shirt. There was a line of sweat around his neckline and his armpits because he'd just worked out on the third floor. His forehead was dotted with perspiration, and his arms were a little thicker than they usually were because the blood was pumping. "Where are you going?"

"To dinner with my family."

He pulled off his clothes and tossed them into the

hamper, stripping down until he was just in his hard and sweaty skin.

I tried not to stare, tried not to think about running my tongue over that hot body.

"Tonight?" he asked.

"Yeah."

"Where?"

"This café a few blocks away."

He stared at me, his soft dick still impressively big even though the rest of his blood had been supplied to his muscles. His displeasure was obvious in the hard lines of his face. "Why?"

"Why what? Are we going to that café? It's good."

"Why are you going out to dinner with them?"

"Because they're my family…"

That obviously wasn't the right answer because he stared at me with more anger. "And who's included in this?"

I felt the anger rise in my blood, felt it slowly start to boil. "I don't appreciate this interrogation. I go where I want to go—and I see who I want to see."

"You should look up the definition of prisoner because you obviously don't know what it means."

"Fuck off."

"How about I fuck you instead?" he countered as he cornered me against the closet, over six feet of pure man. When he was sweaty and hot, it reminded me of the way he looked after he screwed me for a long time. Sweat collected all over his physique, and his skin became slippery over his big muscles. My nails struggled to get a hold because they kept streaking down his wet skin.

"I'm going to dinner with Conway and Sapphire, alright? They worked late in Milan and wanted to see me."

He cocked his head slightly, seeming to not like that answer. "Conway is arrogant like his father. Probably because he looks just like his father."

I'd never let him insult my family without a retaliation. My family was everything to me. Without them, I was nothing. "Conway is not arrogant. He's kind, compassionate, and an extremely successful man. He built his company on his own, not using a dime from my parents. I wish I could say the same. I'm proud to call him my brother."

His blue eyes shifted back and forth as they looked into mine, studying me. "All he cares about is money— like the rest of us. Don't put him on a pedestal. You'll just watch him fall. He's not everything you think he is." His hands pressed against the wall, cornering me against the closet.

"He's my brother. It doesn't matter who he is or what he's done. I love him anyway—because that's what family means. Regardless of what you think he's done, it won't change the way I feel about him. I admire him for his good qualities, and I'll love him no matter what mistakes he's made. That's something you'll never understand…"

That was obviously a poor choice of words, because his angry expression deepened. "Because I don't have a family?"

"No…that's not what I meant. I meant—"

"Don't backpedal. Own up to your crimes—like a real woman." He dropped his arms and stepped back. He turned his back on me, his shoulders shifting as he headed into the bathroom to shower.

"It's really not what I meant."

He grabbed a towel off the dresser. "Then what did you mean? That I'm too heartless and cold to understand what unconditional love is?" He turned around, the white towel gripped in his hand. "If I didn't understand what unconditional love was, then I wouldn't be risking my life to avenge my mother. I wouldn't still love her despite what she did to put food on the table. You think you're so much better than me because you had a perfect life. Well, I've got news for you. You're a spoiled little brat who has no idea what it really means to suffer." He turned his back on me and walked toward the shower, slamming the bathroom door behind him.

I remained in front of the closet and listened to the water start to run. Our relationship was so volatile and unpredictable. One moment, we were pledging our fidelity to one another, and then the next, we were telling each other off. I'd never had a relationship with a man that was so emotional, that changed so drastically from minute to minute because we were both so passionate. We'd had another fight that ripped us apart, but when I came back later that evening, we would have the same unbelievable sex we always did. Maybe the fight made the sex better. Maybe the threat of violence made it deeper. I wasn't sure.

I wasn't sure of anything at this point.

I HUGGED Sapphire first when I reached the table, noting the way her stomach stuck out just slightly. Her belly probably wouldn't be noticeable if she weren't so slender. But since her waistline was so narrow, the outline of her belly was visible through her shirt. "You're showing already."

"I know." She hugged me back before she placed her hand over her belly. "I can't feel anything other than my belly stretching my jeans, but it's still pretty incredible."

I placed my hand on her belly too, feeling nothing like she said. "It's still amazing. There's a little Barsetti in there."

"I know." A glow accompanied her smile. "I've always wanted a family, and now I'm having one."

Conway cleared his throat as he appeared at my side. "Are you going to say hi to me?"

"Can I finish my conversation with Sapphire first?" I countered.

He gave me the same look he'd been giving me my entire life, that look of pure loathing. "You say hello to everyone before you engage in a conversation. I know you're trashy, but have you forgotten all your manners?"

"You think I won't knee you in the groin right here in the restaurant?" I threatened.

"You think I won't slap—"

"Enough," Sapphire said. "Say hello and hug it out."

Conway immediately obeyed, whipped so hard that he wasn't the same man I once knew. He sighed then extended his arms. "Hey, Vanessa. It's nice to see you." He pulled me into his chest and hugged me.

I hugged him back. "You too."

He could insult me as much as he wanted, but when his arms were around me, he hugged me for a long time, telling me he missed me—telling me he loved me.

He pulled away then returned to his seat.

"That's better," Sapphire said. "You two are like fire and gasoline sometimes…"

"We're Barsettis," I said. "Get used to it."

"I'll try," she said with a chuckle. "So what's new with you? Your father said you're dropping out of school to paint full time?"

"Yeah." I told them about my decision and why I'd chosen that route. It was easy to talk to them about art, so I dragged it out as long as possible. I didn't want them to ask me about my personal life. Sapphire and I talked about those things all the time, but I didn't want to mention men around Conway.

Conway always got so weird about it. If he could

put me in an arranged marriage, he would. But if Conway knew about the situation I was in right now, he'd have every right to be livid about it.

"So when's the wedding?" I asked, keeping the conversation focused and away from me.

"Spring," Sapphire said. "The second the snow is gone and the sun is out, we'll do it. I just hope I'm not too big."

"Whatever size you are, you'll look perfect." Conway had his hand on her thigh, and he stared at her just the way my father stared at my mother. Maybe it was because their features were so startlingly similar, but sometimes I felt like I was talking to my father when I was with Conway.

Sapphire didn't smile, but her cheeks filled with a dash of color.

"I'm excited," I said. "It'll be beautiful. What's new with work? Are you not modeling at all anymore?"

"No, not really," Sapphire said. "But Conway has decided to launch a new line of lingerie."

"He's always launching something new."

"But this is a different kind of lingerie," Conway said. "I've basically designed maternity lingerie."

I almost made a disgusted face because I knew exactly what inspired it.

"All men are different, but I think Sapphire is absolutely stunning with that baby bump. And if I feel that way, then other men must too. So I'm launching a sexy line of lingerie for expecting mothers."

"Cool…" I downed my wine to dilute the awkwardness in my stomach. I didn't care that my brother designed lingerie, but I didn't want to hear about his inspiration. It was so gross.

Conway excused himself to the bathroom, leaving us alone.

"I'm sorry if that's weird for you," Sapphire said.

"No, don't worry about it," I said. "I'm glad you guys are happy. My brother's occupation has never bothered me, and don't ever tell him I said this, but I'm really proud of him. He's the best of the best because he's a very successful and intelligent man. But if you ever tell him I said that, I'll deny it until my deathbed."

She chuckled. "Alright."

"I'm happy you guys are in love. I like seeing my brother happy…even if it's a little disgusting."

"You're so mature," she teased. "So…anything going on in your love life?"

"Nope. Nada. Nothing." I fired off my answers so quickly that even I could tell I was lying.

Sapphire cocked an eyebrow. "No dates or anything?"

"Uh, not really. I've just been busy…"

"Busy doing what? You haven't been in school."

This was taking a bad turn. I knew she was suspicious because I used to go out all the time. I met guys often, dated regularly, and I usually had at least one guy on my line. For me to say there was nothing going on was unlikely. "Okay, I'm seeing someone. But I'm not ready to talk about it."

Sapphire immediately moved closer, her eyes lighting up in excitement. "Who is he?"

"I just said I'm not ready to talk about it."

"Why?" she asked. "Is it serious?"

"No," I said with a laugh. "Not serious at all. It's the opposite…"

"So it's just a fling?"

"I guess…but it's been going on for a while."

"How long?"

"Like…two months?"

Sapphire's mouth fell open in shock. "Vanessa, that's not a fling."

"Well, it is," I said quickly. "I wouldn't call it a relationship. It's definitely *not* a relationship. But we just have this passion…this heat. Hands down, he's the best sex I've ever had."

"Wow…"

"And a part of me hates him because I despise his personality and everything about him…but I always wind up in his bed over and over."

"That's where you were, huh?" she asked. "That's why you weren't home?"

"Yes…"

She grinned. "Maybe it'll turn into something more serious."

"No," I said immediately. "It can't. It never will."

"Why are you so certain?"

If only I could tell her. "We aren't really compatible in other ways…the only thing that's keeping us together is the sex."

"Sex is important."

"But it's not everything…" A part of me did like his other qualities, like his loyalty and his protectiveness. He loved his mother despite her immoral career choice, and that made me respect him. He listened to me when I asked him to. He was always honest with me, and people were rarely honest. But he wanted nothing more than to wipe out my family line.

"But it could turn into everything. With Conway…" She shut her mouth and suppressed her grin. "Never mind. Too weird."

"Yeah…too weird."

"I'm just saying…if you have the passion, maybe you have everything else too."

No. I was stuck in a serious kidnapping situation, and I was fucking this man to keep him away from my family. That was the basis of our relationship, and it would end as badly as it started. I spotted Conway coming back to the table from across the room. "We'll see."

"I want an update, Vanessa."

"Alright. But keep this to yourself."

"Of course."

CONWAY INSISTED on taking me home even though I told him I would take a cab. It was past seven in the evening, so there was no way I could ask him to drop me off at Bones's place. How would I explain that?

After five minutes of arguing, I finally got into the car, and he took me back to my apartment. He held Sapphire's hand on the middle console, his fingers pressed in between hers. He drove with one hand on the wheel, taking peeks at his fiancée from time to time.

Looking at them made me jealous. Jealous that I wouldn't live long enough to find something like that. I was in the most passionate relationship I'd ever had, but it had no foundation of friendship or love.

It was just violence and sex.

My phone vibrated in my pocket with a text message. I pulled it out to see a message from Bones. *Where are you going?*

You're such a stalker.

Where are you going?

He would just keep asking the question until he got the answer he was looking for. *My place.*

Your ass belongs over here.

Conway wouldn't let me take a cab. And I couldn't have him drop me off at your place.

Why not?

I rolled my eyes. *Good night. I'll see you tomorrow.*

He didn't write back.

Conway dropped me off five minutes later, and he

locked the car at the street with Sapphire inside before he walked me to the door.

"You don't need to walk me to the door. We aren't high school kids on a date."

"You're my little sister. I'm gonna walk you to the door even if you're eighty, alright?" He leaned against the door and watched me unlock it.

But it wasn't locked.

I tried to play it cool and pretend everything was normal. "Thanks for dinner. I'll see you later."

"Night." He brought me into his chest and hugged me.

My brother and I never hugged, unless it was a holiday or something. "You've been hugging me a lot lately…"

"I almost lost you. Made me realize I shouldn't be such an ass to you."

"You were an ass to me earlier."

"You know what I mean." He pulled away, giving me a thoughtful expression the same way my father did. "I just worry about you. After what happened, I'm scared leaving you here by yourself. Now that you aren't going to school, maybe you should live with us. You can't beat the view."

I knew Conway didn't want me there, so his fear for my safety outweighed his need for privacy. "That's sweet…but I'm fine here."

"Are you sure?"

If only he knew what was really going on. It would

break his heart, which was why I never wanted to tell him. "I'm sure, Con. Really, don't worry about me. I'm a tough girl."

"Woman," he corrected. "You're a tough woman. Sometimes I forget how strong you are, and then I see you in action and realize how incredible you are. That makes me feel better, but then I start to worry again. I can't wait until you get married. I never thought I'd say that, but it would make my life easier."

"You growl anytime a man goes near me."

"I know…" He rolled his eyes. "I just want the right guy to go near you. I want you to marry a guy who can take care of you."

"I don't need a man to take care of me. I can take care of myself."

"You know what I mean, Vanessa. It would give me peace of mind knowing you lived with a huge guy who could scare off anyone that looked at you twice…just the way I do with Sapphire."

Little did he know I already had that, but my protector was also my murderer.

"I hope you find that soon…so Father and I can relax."

"You'd find something else to get worked up over." I tried to keep the conversation light because his words were killing me. My brother loved me so much and worried about me. He would do anything for me, and right now, I was trapped. I was trapped, and he couldn't help me even if he wanted to. I was protecting him, making sure Bones never laid a hand on him or Sapphire. But Conway had no knowledge of the sacrifice I was making.

And I wanted it to stay that way.

He smiled before he placed his hand on my shoulder. "Call me if you need anything, alright?"

"Alright."

"I mean it. And if you change your mind about living with us, let me know."

"I won't change my mind, but thanks anyway."

He finally walked away and took the stairs back to the car at the curb.

I stepped inside my apartment, letting my face fall back into its look of sorrow. I was back to my prison, back to my cage.

In the shadows, I saw Bones sitting on the couch. Fully dressed with his blue eyes focused on me, he stared at me from his spot in the darkness.

"How the hell did you get here so fast?"

The only response I got was a cold look from his icy eyes.

"Forget it…I don't care anyway." I walked past him and headed to my bedroom, the ache in my chest too much to carry. It was the second time my brother was right next to Bones without even realizing it.

I didn't like them being so close together.

I tore off my clothes and immediately got into bed, even though it was only eight in the evening. It was way too early to go to sleep, but I had no motivation to watch TV or do anything else. I just wanted to lie there, to let myself be swallowed by my own self-pity.

His footsteps sounded in the doorway, and then his clothes started to hit the floor.

I wanted him to leave, but I also wanted him to stay. He was the source of my misery, but he also had the power to make me feel better. When his strong arms were wrapped around me, I felt like nothing could hurt me. He lit a fire in my veins, made me yearn for him in a way I never yearned for anyone else. His hard chest and strong-beating heart consoled all my terrors. When our bodies were connected and my fingers were digging into his back, all the bad thoughts stopped. There were no thoughts at all. It was just the two of us.

His heavy body shifted the mattress as he maneuvered beside me. He pressed his chest against my back and wrapped his arm around my waist. His head moved to the back of my neck and he breathed gently, his warm breaths drifting across my skin.

My arm rested over his, feeling the powerful heat his body projected.

He pressed a kiss to the back of my neck, his lips soft against my cold skin.

Like our earlier fight never happened, we lay there in comfortable silence. Like my brother and I didn't just have a moment right outside the front door, we lay there like lovers. I knew Bones had overheard the entire conversation if he was sitting on the couch the whole time, but he didn't say anything about it.

"Baby." His masculine voice filled the darkness of my bedroom.

I turned my head toward him, my eyes moving to the ceiling without turning around. "Hmm?"

"Tell me what you want."

I faced forward again. "Nothing. I just want to stay like this."

"Do you want me to leave?"

He'd never given me the option before. "Does it matter? Would you go if I asked?"

He kissed my shoulder. "Yes."

This was my chance to get rid of him, but I didn't take it. I didn't want to lie in that bed by myself. I was used to his big body beside me. I slept with him every single night, so when he wasn't there, my night was always terrible. "I want you to stay…"

He kissed my shoulder again, giving me his tongue. He moved up my neck until he reached the shell of my ear. "Then I'll stay."

I SAT at the easel and continued working on the painting. I'd taken a photo when I walked home from the store. It was an image of an alleyway, a narrow place that had a few bicycles leaned up against the walls. It was an iconic image of Italian culture, so I snapped it on my phone and then got to work.

Now I was almost done.

I sat in my workspace, the room Bones had given to me. He rarely came in here while I worked, giving me my space so I could be creative without hindrance. The painting I made for him was still in here, leaning against the wall because he hadn't found a place for it yet.

At midday, my wrist started to ache, so I took a break and walked into the kitchen.

The kitchen table was covered with paperwork, guns, and ammunition. Semiautomatic weapons along with pistols and shotguns were on the surface, surrounded by rounds of ammunition. Bones stood there, wearing a t-shirt and black jeans. He didn't look up at me when I walked in, his arms crossed over his chest and his eyes focused.

I could grab any one of those and shoot him between the eyes.

It was tempting—just for a second. "What's all this about?"

He took a few seconds before he finally turned his head my way. "Work."

"Work? It looks like you're about to take out a whole country."

"I'm hitting Joe tonight."

He hadn't mentioned it in a few days so I had hoped he'd dropped this vendetta. Bones was a smart man, but his stubbornness would get him killed. He needed to learn to release these grudges and move on with his life. He lived in the past way too much. "I was hoping you'd let this go…"

"Do I ever let anything go?" he challenged.

I stared at the shotgun sitting on the table. "Are these loaded?"

"Yes." He kept his arms crossed over his chest and stared at me, slightly amused.

"And you're just going to leave these out like this?"

"Yes." His confidence suggested he didn't think I was a threat.

"You shouldn't be so arrogant."

He grabbed the shotgun sitting in front of him then popped open the barrel. It was full of rounds. He shut it again then placed it on the table right in front of me. "Take your shot, baby. I'm a strong man, but against a shotgun, I have no chance." He stared me down and waited for me to do something."

I wanted to wipe that smug look off his face and shoot him right between the eyes. All I had to do was grab the gun and aim. But even if I had the strength to do it, the table was full of loaded guns. He was a lot faster than me, so all he had to do was grab a pistol and shoot me in the chest.

If that weren't the case, I might have done something.

I turned around and walked into the kitchen.

"That's what I thought."

I stopped in my tracks and turned back around, my eyes full of warning.

He maintained his arrogant expression.

"You've kept me for over two months, and I'm still

here. So drop that stupid look and make good on your threat." I grabbed the shotgun and placed it in front of him.

Instantly, his smile was gone.

"Come on. Do it." Both of my hands gripped the table as I leaned over. "What are you waiting for? Take me out and then kill Joe. Your vendettas will be over, and you can go back to your lonely and pathetic life."

The anger rose into his shoulders, but he still didn't grab the gun.

"That's what I thought." I turned my back to him, exposing myself completely, and walked into the kitchen. I shut down his arrogance and reminded him that he was just as weak as I was. He said he was going to kill me, but the more time passed, the more I thought he wouldn't. He listened to my brother on my doorstep, and he protected me when he didn't have to. This relationship wasn't black and white anymore. He thought he had power over me.

I had the same power over him.

His footsteps thudded hard against the floor, telling me he was stampeding this way.

I barely had time to turn around before he scooped me into his arms and lifted me onto the counter. He crushed his mouth against mine, and he kissed me so hard I could barely breathe. His shirt came over his head and fell on the tile, and then his pants and boxers were pushed down so his cock could be free.

Like all the other times, my body was lit on fire, and

I was kissing him back. My hands groped his hard body, and I panted into his mouth. My nails clawed at him, and I lifted my body so I could help him get my panties off. My shirt was pulled to my waist, and then he was inside me with one hard thrust.

"God…" I gripped his shoulders and held on as he fucked me on the counter, his hips moving hard to get me deep and good. My knees were bent, and my ankles dug into his back as I held on. My face was pressed into his neck while he thrust over and over, claiming me as his and making sure I wouldn't forget it.

"Tell me you're mine." He pulled his face away so he could look me in the eye. His face was so furious, furious at listening to me speak to him that way. His blue eyes seemed gray because they lost their beauty. Full of rage and aggression, he took on a different appearance.

I defied him, refusing to say the words he wanted to hear. My nails dug into him harder, and I enjoyed how big his cock felt inside me, how much it stretched me. He fucked me better than any other man had fucked me, did it with such possessiveness and rawness. Even if I survived this, I would never find a man who could replace him. I'd still touch myself to his memory, even years down the line. But I wouldn't say those words out loud.

He stopped thrusting, letting his big cock sit inside me. He breathed in my face, taking away the pleasure he just gave me. "Say it."

I didn't want to say it. I refused to say it.

He started to move slowly, giving me his big dick before pulling out again. He kissed me, giving me his tongue and his passion. He made me feel so good, even at a slow pace. Then he stopped again, taking away the pleasure between my legs. "Say it."

My head was in the clouds, and now all I cared about was the pleasure between my legs. I said what I didn't want to say. And it hurt because I knew it was true. I'd been his for over two months, and I would always be his. "I'm yours."

He didn't smile in arrogance, but his eyes darkened in approval. He fucked me hard once more, rewarding me for my obedience. He gave it to me good, making me moan and claw at his back. I could feel the orgasm approaching, feeling my pussy tightening.

And then it hit me like a freight train, so powerful that it was unexpected. I bit his shoulder as I came all over his dick, enjoying the powerful climax that he gave me with such ease. He'd been fucking me for so long that he knew exactly how to make me come, and how to do it so easily.

The shame rushed through me, but it didn't compare to the pleasure.

He looked into my eyes, the arrogance in full force. "That's what I thought."

I WATCHED TV in bed and waited for him to join me after he finished in his office.

But he never came.

I should just go to sleep, but it was difficult to get comfortable without him. Now I needed his hard chest, his warmth, and his beating heart as a lullaby. I left the bedroom and went to his office in search of him, wearing his t-shirt.

He wasn't there.

I walked into the living room and found him sitting on the couch, loading his pistol with a black leather bag on the table.

So he was really doing it.

I stopped next to the couch, my arms across my chest. "You're really doing this?"

He cocked the gun. "Yes." He clicked the safety then set it on the table. "I'll be back tomorrow afternoon."

"And what if you don't come back?"

He lifted his gaze to look at me. "I will."

"You shouldn't be so arrogant all the time. Arrogance leads to mistakes."

"I don't make mistakes. And that's why I'm arrogant."

I shouldn't bother with this conversation because I didn't care anyway. "Whatever. Good luck." I sat on the other couch, my arms still crossed over my chest.

He stood up and placed his pistol in the holster. Then he pulled the strap over his shoulder.

I had a bad feeling about tonight that I couldn't explain. When he left on his other missions, I was never worried about him coming back. But since this was personal, I was afraid it would cloud his judgment and make him do something stupid.

He stared down at me, his broad shoulders thick in the black jacket he wore. "What is it?"

I stood up, keeping my arms tight around his body. "Let it go, Bones. Just—"

"No." He walked to the elevator, dismissing the conversation.

I stared at his back, my heart moving into my throat.

He hit the button and waited for the doors to open. They came apart, but instead of stepping to leave, he turned back around and stared at me. He looked at me with those beautiful blue eyes, but they weren't so pretty when they were filled with such hatred.

I didn't want to say goodbye to him. If he died, it would make my life easier. Maybe Joe would do the dirty work for me. But I was lying to myself. If Bones died trying to avenge his mother, I wouldn't sweep it under the rug. I wouldn't return to my apartment like nothing happened.

It would hurt.

I crossed the distance between us and stopped in front of him, my heart racing in my chest. I didn't lower my arms because I didn't want to welcome him into my body. But I was already standing there, giving myself to him. I lifted my chin and looked him in the eye. "You promised me you wouldn't leave me…"

He cupped my cheeks with both of his hands and looked into my face, his eyes softening once he looked at the vulnerability in mine. "I know."

"Then keep your promise."

He pressed his forehead to mine before he kissed the corner of my mouth. "I will, baby."

4

Bones

The job was easy.

After he left the opera, he would head to the brothel a few streets away. Max told me he had an appointment there, with a busty brunette he frequented.

Apparently, she wasn't on his kill list.

I sat in the black car at the curb, all the windows tinted and dark. It was a burner car, meaning I'd stolen it from the sidewalk, and I would ditch it somewhere random. They wouldn't be able to trace anything back to me.

Not that there would be anyone left alive to find me.

The building looked abandoned, the windows carefully boarded up so not even a hint of light escaped. There was no movement on the streets around, no pedestrians or anything. Only powerful men walked through the front door because they didn't care if they were caught walking inside.

Only cowardly men used the back entrance, the ones with wives who couldn't know about their dirty secrets. I'd paid for whores, but I never went to establishments like this. I never went anywhere public where people would see my face.

Not because I had anything to hide.

I waited in the car with my gun at the ready, the silencer over the barrel so I could do this quietly. I'd prefer to do this in private so I could torture the guy, but luck wasn't on my side. Since there wasn't a pot of gold at the end of this mission, my crew thought the risk outweighed the reward.

I didn't take it personally. This vendetta was my own thing. If Max asked me to do something like this for him, I probably would have done the same thing. Even if I killed this guy and all his men, it wouldn't change anything.

She was still dead.

It was the coldhearted truth.

I sat in silence and waited, listening for sounds and searching for headlights. I preoccupied myself with thinking of what Vanessa had said to me before I left. She wanted me to come back.

She made me promise I would.

Our relationship was so fucked up. I didn't even know what we were anymore. She was my enemy and I was hers, but neither one of us wanted to kill each other. I kept telling myself when the time came I would pull the trigger.

But I was starting to think that was bullshit.

Maybe I could achieve my vendetta differently. Maybe I could kill her entire family but keep her as a prisoner anyway. That way I could spare her life and keep her as a slave.

But I knew if I really wiped out her entire family, she would never fuck me again.

She really would kill me.

The only way to keep her this way, keep her passionate and affectionate, was to keep things the way they were.

But I knew I couldn't keep it up forever.

And I certainly couldn't let her go or drop this blood feud. That wasn't an option. Which led me back to my original conclusion.

I had to kill her.

There was no way around it.

But damn, when she was needy and clingy, I loved it.

I loved it so damn much.

I'd never find another woman to fill my bed the way she did. I would never have another woman who could take my fat dick the way she could. I would never have a woman slap me like that, who had the balls to stand up to me even though I was more than twice her size. They didn't make women like that anymore.

How could I kill a woman like that?

I had to stop thinking about it. The more I thought about it, the harder it would be. It didn't matter how much I loved being between her legs. I wasn't going to be a pussy and chicken out. I had to kill her the way I vowed I would.

Otherwise, what kind of man would I be?

I just had to enjoy her while I could and put up that painting after she was dead.

Headlights approached in the distance, and I knew it was time for action.

It was an SUV, all black with black windows. It pulled up right to the curb, and then a man hopped out of the passenger side and opened the back door so Joe could get out.

Here we go.

I jumped out of the driver's door and opened fire.

I shot the man who opened the door for Joe, hitting him right in the skull so he went down like a potato sack.

With lightning speed, another man hopped out of the other side, a semiautomatic in his hands. He opened fire, and I dodged out of the way before he could hit me. I landed a few bullets his way, hitting him twice in the chest.

He didn't go down, probably because of a bullet-proof vest.

I got hit three times right in the heart, but my vest protected me. I finally got him down, but Joe opened fire. His driver did the same.

I moved behind another car and took cover while they shattered the windows. I waited for them to burn through their rounds before I took aim again. I reloaded then fired again, destroying the doors to the SUV.

Another car sped down the road, the headlights becoming visible. He halted to a stop, and more men got out.

Shit.

He had had more backup.

Fuck, I was outnumbered. Even I couldn't do this.

I pulled the grenade from my pouch and threw it at the SUV.

They all ran for cover.

I sprinted into the alleyway, but not before I took a bullet to the arm.

"Fuck." I didn't slow down, sprinting hard and making more blood ooze from the wound because my heart was working so fast.

I knew these streets better than they did since I'd slept on these sidewalks. So I cut across different alleyways and took alternate roads, even the ones that had been torn up and closed for decades.

I was losing a lot of blood and growing weaker by the second.

I wanted to call for backup but I couldn't.

I couldn't drag Max into this.

So I kept going until I found the right place to hide. I ripped off my shirt underneath my sweater and vest and secured my wound, applying as much pressure as I could. Then I turned off my cell so they couldn't find the signal as they searched the streets for me.

I'd be there until morning. And maybe even longer.

I LAID low until the following evening.

When the night was at its deepest, I got into a taxi and headed back to my apartment.

I didn't catch sight of any of Joe's men.

They must have assumed I got away and gave up. They would try to figure out who I was, but other than seeing glimpses of my face in the dark, they didn't have much to go off of. I didn't leave anything behind in the car, and the car wasn't even mine.

But it would make it much more difficult to kill him now.

He'd be waiting for me.

My sweater covered my injury so no one would know I'd been shot. Black was a great color to wear if you were trying to hide blood. But the bullet was painful, and I'd lost more blood than I should have. I needed to remove the artifact from my body and have it properly dressed.

And I needed antibiotics—immediately.

If it grew into an infection, then I would have a serious problem.

Going to any hospital wasn't an option. Joe's men would be checking the records every hour, hoping I would show up.

I was just around the corner from my place when I thought of Vanessa.

She must be worried out of her mind. She made me promise I'd come back.

I always kept my promises. Soon enough, she would see. I wondered what her face would look like. Would there be tears? Would she be angry? Would she fuck me harder than she ever had before because she was relieved I was back?

Or would she just be disappointed instead?

Disappointed that I hadn't died.

The thought hurt more than I wanted it to.

When I finally arrived at my place, I took the elevator to my floor. The doors opened, and I found Vanessa standing right in the entryway, her eyes red and puffy from not sleeping. She was still in the same clothes she'd been wearing when I'd left. The second she laid eyes on me, her hands moved through her hair, and she breathed a sigh of relief so loud it could reach through solid glass. "You fucking asshole. You told me you would be back by the afternoon at the latest. It's almost midnight. You didn't call, you didn't text, nothing. How could you——"

"I'm here." I cupped her cheeks and kissed her, caring more about that mouth than the gunshot wound in my bicep. My fingers dug into her hair even though they were dirty and smelled like metal from the gun. My lips moved with hers, bringing her down to a sense of calm. "Baby, I always keep my promises."

She pulled away from my lips and looked at me, still angry but not as much as before. "What happened? Why are you home so late? Did something go wrong?"

I got hard watching the concern spread across her face. She couldn't downplay her worry in the moment, not when she was so relieved I was back. If this were a different situation, she would have hidden her true feelings as much as possible. But right now, she simply couldn't do it.

"Stop smiling like that. This isn't funny."

"I'm laughing."

"But you're grinning like there's something humorous about this situation." Her green eyes flashed with ferocity. "You went to kill someone, and when you didn't come back…I thought you might never come back."

"And wouldn't that be a good thing?"

She shut her mouth, the shame creeping across her face. If I died, her family would be safe. But she couldn't stop herself from wanting me to be alive, from wanting me to be safe. Her emotions were ripping apart in two very different directions. She still struggled to make sense of them.

Just as I did. I pulled my sweater over my head and dropped it on the ground. It was soaked in too much blood, so now it was ruined.

When her eyes saw the blood on my arm and the t-shirt wrapped around the wound, she covered her mouth with both hands. "Jesus…"

"I need your help again. You know what to do."

"We need to take you to a hospital."

"No." I opened the cabinet and pulled out the first aid kit. It was packed with everything I needed, because this wasn't my first time getting shot. I sat on the couch and opened the kit. I pulled the t-shirt off before I poured vodka over the wound.

It burned like a bitch.

"Bones…" Vanessa sat beside me, pain in her eyes. "We should get you to a doctor."

"I said no."

"I have no medical training. You've lost so much blood—"

"I've lost more before." I handed her the tweezers. "You should be a pro at this by now."

She gave up the argument when she knew I wouldn't be changing my mind. She grabbed my elbow and then dug the metal into my wound. She found the small bullet after a few seconds then carefully removed it.

It hurt more than the vodka, but I didn't show a hint of my discomfort.

She set the bullet on the table, covered in blood. "What happened?" She poured more alcohol over the wound then grabbed the needle and thread.

"I took out a few of his men, and it was going like I thought it would. But he had backup I didn't know about. I was outnumbered, and I didn't have enough rounds to compete. So I tossed a grenade and ran for it. I got shot before I made it to the alleyway."

She concentrated on threading my wound closed, but she couldn't mask her terror. "So you didn't kill him?"

I hated admitting the truth out loud. I hated admitting I failed. "No."

"I'm sorry…" She kept threading, getting half the wound closed in a few minutes. "What now?"

"I'll have to keep a low profile for a while before I try again."

Her hands stopped working. "You're kidding me, right?"

I stared straight ahead, ignoring her pissed look. "You know I have to kill him."

"Well, obviously, you can't. You're just going to get yourself killed." She raised her voice, yelling at me as she held the needle and thread. "That's the dumbest thing I've ever heard. I've never met a man more stubborn—"

I kissed her because it was the only way I could shut her up.

It worked—like always.

I pulled away and gave her an authoritative look with my eyes. "I know I am. And you're probably right, it will get me killed. But it's my decision. Now stitch me up, and let's move on."

She stared at me like she might say something, but then she thought the better of it and finished the job.

"The times when my parents are the angriest at me is when I put myself in dangerous situations. I snuck out one night when I was sixteen and went driving with some friends. When my father found out…" She shook her head. "I can't remember the last time I'd seen him that angry. There were no boys involved and we weren't drinking and driving, but he was furious that I was out alone with a bunch of girls in the middle of the night in Florence."

"Why are you telling me this?"

"Because it's every parents' worst nightmare for their child to put themselves in danger. She did the best she could to protect you and raise you, to give you a better life than she had. And you're doing a piss-poor job of showing your gratitude."

VANESSA FOCUSED on her artwork during the day, doing her best to ignore me while the sun was up. She was pissed at me for a lot of reasons, but her biggest reason of all at the moment was because I'd been shot.

She could barely look at me.

But when the sun was gone and the lights were out, she was as needy and affectionate as she'd always been. She fucked me harder than I fucked her, needing all of me to reach her climax. She clawed at me, whispered promises to me while I was deep inside her. Our connection was borderline spiritual, and we moved together like we were of one mind.

We were of one mind.

But once the sun was up, she acted like she hated me again.

That was fine. I hated her too.

I walked into the art room and saw the collection of paintings she'd made in the past few weeks. The one she painted of herself was still my favorite, a piece of artwork I would never sell, no matter the price. It was so moody, dark, and sexy. It captured the way I felt about her perfectly. It was complicated, emotional, and sad. It illustrated my view of her, the exact way I stared at Vanessa every single day.

She had other paintings that she'd completed, all leaning against the wall. They all contained images of Milan and Tuscany, all beautiful in their unique ways. Before long, she would have plenty of artwork to fill an entire gallery.

I noticed one painting had been turned the opposite way. It leaned against the wall, the paint hidden from view. I walked toward it, curious to see what Vanessa was hiding.

"No." Her voice steadied me, full of authority and foreign power.

I stopped and turned my head toward her.

She sat on the stool, her black hair pulled back and a drop of blue paint on her nose. She was working on a golden field of sunflowers. She held the brush between her fingertips, a mixture of yellow and white paint on the tip. "That's private."

"Nothing is private here, not when I own everything." I reached for it again.

"Off-limits." She set the brush on the easel and hopped off the stool, her short legs only touching the ground once she was on her feet. "I mean it." She grabbed me by the arm and yanked me away.

Like she had enough strength to make me do anything. I let her pull me, only because this painting seemed particularly important to her. "Tell me why, and I'll think about it."

"It's private," she repeated.

"You have to give me a better reason than that."

"It's just…" Her eyes moved down. "I'm just not ready. I don't even know why I painted it."

"You're only making me more interested."

"Just leave it alone, alright?" Her eyes flicked back to mine, green and beautiful. "I've pulled two bullets out of your arm and stitched you up twice. The least you could do is leave this alone."

"You put one of the bullets there, in case you forgot."

"And don't expect me to apologize for it because I never will."

There was my baby. I tried to hide my smile. "I want to see it eventually."

"Fine."

"Then why can't I see it now?"

"I just don't want you to." She wore the white smock to cover her clothes, but even the shapeless fabric couldn't diminish her unquestionable beauty. "It's personal, and I'm not ready to explain myself or try to understand what I painted. Just drop it."

"You really aren't helping…"

"Let it go, Bones." She returned to the easel and grabbed her brushes and set them in the water glass. Her painting was only halfway completed, but she didn't seem motivated to finish it that evening.

I glanced at the painting again, more intrigued than ever before. I could just tell her she didn't have any rights and do whatever I wanted, but her artwork was important to her. It was like seeing a piece of her soul. If she didn't want me to have it, I couldn't force it. Just like when it came to fucking—she had to decide.

"How's your arm?" She peeled off her smock. The sun was going down, so she was becoming less hostile. As the night deepened, she couldn't restrain her affection. Her kisses started, and then she would move into my lap and take it a step further until we were in bed together, rocking the headboard all night long.

"Don't even notice it." That wasn't true. It was sore, and it ached when I put weight on it. I held myself on top of her every night but ignored the pain because my cock was in heaven inside that wet slit. I concentrated on her kiss and her awesome tits, not the pain in my arm. I usually swallowed a handful of pills before bed then I was good.

"Good. It seems to be healing nicely…" She finished putting away her supplies then glanced at herself in the mirror. She wiped away the dot of blue paint then headed to the door. "I'm getting cabin fever. I've been working on my art all week and haven't stepped outside once."

I usually made dinner for us every night because she didn't know how to cook and never cared to learn. But maybe she needed a change of scenery. "How about we go to dinner tonight?" We'd only been to breakfast once, and that didn't go over well.

"Like, you and me?" she asked incredulously.

"Yes. Man and woman."

"In public?"

"Yes."

She rolled her eyes. "Not a good idea."

"Why?"

"Conway and Carter are in the city a lot."

"So?"

"Imagine if they saw me with you."

"You think I care?" I hoped I ran into them. It would be a nice coincidence.

"I know they don't know who you are, but I don't want them to see me with a man. They'll ask me a million questions—"

"Conway knows who I am."

She stilled by the doorway. "He does?"

I nodded.

"Are you sure?"

"Absolutely. He sat right beside me at the Underground. And even though I was trying out a disguise, one of the Skull Kings called me by my name. There was no way Conway would just ignore that piece of information—and I know he heard it."

"If my family knew who you were, they would have killed you by now."

That was my assumption too, but an attack never came. "They don't know what my motives are. So instead of provoking me, they're choosing to remain ambivalent and hope we can coexist peacefully."

"Shows how little they know…"

"Couldn't agree more. You should always take out your enemy before they can take you out."

"Or you should take advantage of the fact that my family are peaceful people who have no ill will toward you. You should just let the dust remain settled and move on with your life. You provoked Joe Pedretti and almost died, and fucking with my family will certainly kill you."

"You underestimate me, baby."

She rolled her eyes. "Your stubbornness will get you killed. I guess if I wait long enough, it'll happen on its own."

"Judging by your reaction to my gunshot wound, you wouldn't be too happy about that."

She shot me a glare before she stormed off. "I'll pass on dinner, but I'm going out anyway."

I followed her into the hallway. "You aren't going out without me."

"Watch me." She went into the bedroom and opened her closet. She grabbed a backless black dress with black heels.

She wasn't going out dressed like that—not without me.

She changed her outfit, pulling on the skintight dress and heels.

I changed into slacks and a dark blue collared shirt, one of the nicest things I owned. I had a few suits, but I hardly ever wore them.

She fixed her hair and freshened her makeup. "I'm going out alone, Bones. I need to get some fresh air—away from you."

"Either we go together, or you don't go at all." I pulled on my dress shoes and tied the shoelaces before I rose to my feet.

She eyed me up and down, checking me out but doing her best to hide it.

"What's it going to be, baby?"

She walked out of the bedroom, her luscious ass shaking. "Fine. But let's go somewhere low-key."

"I know just the place."

I TOOK her to one of the most expensive restaurants in Milan, a place with a three-month waiting list. I'd never been there without the restaurant being packed, crowded with people who'd traveled all the way across Europe just to try their exquisite delicacies.

I didn't have a reservation, but that didn't matter.

No one said no to me.

We sat at a table in the corner, a low-burning candle in the center. Drinking wine was more appropriate for a place like this, but I refused to drink anything but scotch. She would have wine, something from her family's winery, no doubt.

And she did.

The waiter returned with the drinks then took our order before he disappeared.

"So much for low-key," she said as she looked around.

"I wanted to take you somewhere nice."

"Why?"

My eyes moved down her body as I drank my scotch. "Because you look like that."

"So if I dressed like a hag, we would have gone to McDonald's?"

The corner of my mouth rose in a smile, loving her smartass attitude. "Would you rather go to McDonald's?"

"If no one recognizes me there, then yes."

I glanced around the restaurant. "No one knows you are. So you can calm down."

"My father knows a lot of people in the wine business. If they see me here with some guy, they might pass it along to my father. And if they say your name is Bones…then I'm in deep shit."

"That would work out well for me."

Her eyes narrowed.

"Not everyone knows me by name, more by reputation. So even if that did happen, I doubt they know who I am."

She released the breath she was holding, like that made her feel a little better.

"But you shouldn't be so ashamed of me. I'm the best-looking guy in here." I grinned, knowing that arrogant comment would only make her anger rise.

"We both know you are. But that's not the problem."

My smile disappeared, surprised by the words that flew out of her mouth. She said it with such conviction, like she wasn't thinking before she spoke. I knew she was attracted to me. I didn't need to listen to her say that to know it was true. Her wet pussy told me everything I needed to know. But listening to her say it so effortlessly made my cock start to harden in my slacks.

She took a long drink from her wine, like she regretted what she'd just said.

I watched her from across the table, transfixed by her beauty. She wasn't just the most beautiful woman in the restaurant, but the most beautiful woman ever to have walked in there. Now she sat across from me— because she was mine. Her halter top revealed the deep plunge of her cleavage, the gorgeous olive skin that begged for my tongue. Her hair was pulled back elegantly, revealing the nice contours of her face. She had rounded shoulders, toned from using her arms so much in her work. I couldn't see her legs under the table, but I knew they looked absolutely stunning tonight.

And she was all mine.

I drank from my glass, my lips savoring the liquor. I imagined pouring it directly onto her pussy and drinking it all away. I imagined my wet lips sucking her nipples until they were raw. She said she needed to get out because she felt trapped in my apartment.

But I felt trapped when I couldn't fuck her whenever I wanted.

She held her glass as she looked around at the other tables, staring at the couples and families as they enjoyed their dinner. She chose a glass of red wine, a dry blend to complement the steak she ordered. Her eyes turned back to me, and she set her glass down. "What?"

I didn't blink.

"Why are you staring at me like that?"

"You know why." My eyes were doors to my thoughts, and my thoughts weren't difficult to decipher, especially when they were so plainly written on my face. I wasn't a complicated man, and my thoughts were simple. There were only a handful of things I thought about, and there were even fewer things I thought about when it came to Vanessa. Everything was reduced to sex and violence.

She drank from her glass and brushed off my comment subtly, pretending it didn't affect her as deeply as it really did. But we both knew she loved to be the object of my obsession. If I went home with a different woman, it would kill her. The jealousy would eat her alive, and she'd lash out at me, fists flying. If my wound became lethal, she'd beat me too. We despised each other, but we were both being forced to face the hard truth.

We couldn't live without each other.

Dinner was served, and we ate in silence, not exchanging conversation the way most people did. Vanessa and I could say nothing at all, and we'd be at the same level of comfort. An exchange of eye contact was more than enough.

She needed to get out of the apartment, but it resulted in the same situation. We didn't care about anything around us but each other. We didn't speak to anyone or even make eye contact with the waiter. She stared at my body like she couldn't wait to dig her nails into my muscles, and I did the same.

She said she was worried about my gunshot wound, but I think it turned her on.

Bullets killed lesser men. But all they did was slow me down.

Vanessa was a strong woman, so she must be attracted to strong men. I fit that description perfectly, even if I wasn't the most moral person. I did criminal things, but that didn't lessen my strength and protectiveness.

I overheard Conway tell her exactly what he wanted, to have her marry a strong man who could take care of her.

I fit the bill.

She knew it.

I knew it.

We finished dinner then Vanessa excused herself to the restroom.

I got the bill and paid with cash—because I paid for everything with cash. I was eager to leave that public establishment and get back to my place. I preferred Vanessa in just her panties and in my bed. In a restaurant, all the men could look at her. I had to pretend to be okay with it—even though I wasn't.

She was mine.

A brunette walked over to me, her eyes making contact with mine. She was sitting at a table with a few other girls, and as she came closer, she smiled like she knew exactly who I was.

I didn't recognize her.

She stopped at my table. "Hey, B. How are you?"

Her face still wasn't ringing a bell, but she obviously knew who I was. When I picked up women out on the town, I couldn't introduce myself as Bones—not without looking like a weirdo. So I went with the first letter in the name. I told them I had a crazy long name that no one could pronounce, so I stuck with B. "Good. How are you, sweetheart?"

"Great. I'm out with some friends tonight. When I saw you over here, I just wanted to say hi."

No one just wanted to say hi. She wanted something from me. Since I still didn't know who she was, I assumed we'd slept together one time and then moved on. Maybe she was interested in another round. If Vanessa walked out of the bathroom and saw this, she'd flip.

I grinned at the thought. "Thanks for stopping by. Hope you have a good night. I'm just waiting for my wife to come out of the bathroom." I thought I would be a nice guy and get rid of her so she didn't have to deal with Vanessa.

I knew my baby was a little crazy when it came to me.

"Oh…you're married?" she blurted. "I…I didn't see a ring."

I looked at my left hand and made a fist. "I don't usually wear one with my line of work." My eyes glanced to the bathroom, and I saw Vanessa step out, all curves in her tight black dress. Her eyes scanned the room then settled on me with the brunette. It took her a few seconds to deduce what was going on.

Yep, she was pissed.

I couldn't wipe the smug look off my face. "Have a good night. My wife is on her way now, and she's the jealous type…"

"Oh, gotcha." She gave me a smile then walked back to her table to her friends.

She never told me her name.

Just as she walked away, Vanessa arrived and dropped into her chair. With pursed lips, irritated eyes, and a mood that could black out the sun, she wasn't pleased by what she'd just seen. "Hitting on a man when his date goes to the restroom…real classy."

I couldn't even pretend not to enjoy this. "Your face is getting so red."

"Is not," she said defensively. "I just don't appreciate people who pull that stunt."

"What makes you so certain she was even hitting on me?"

She rolled her eyes. "Cut the shit."

I got hard in my slacks watching how upset she got. She was even more possessive of me than I was of her.

"Let's go." She rose to her feet and snuck a look at the brunette who'd made a pass at me, who happened to be looking this way.

When I was out of my chair, Vanessa grabbed my hand and interlocked our fingers together as she walked out of the restaurant. She'd never shared affection with me publicly, and we certainly had never held hands, but now our fingers came together. My hand was twice as big as hers, but they still lined up the right way. She pulled me out of the restaurant, like a horse pulling a carriage ten times its weight.

How could I not enjoy this little tantrum? It was hilarious.

We made it outside then walked to my truck, still holding hands. The brunette was long gone, but Vanessa didn't hold her embrace.

"Are you always this jealous?"

"I'm not jealous."

I cocked an eyebrow, seeing the way her nostrils were still flaring. "I thought you were going to throw a fist back there."

"I should…to teach her some class. You don't go after a man when his woman is in the bathroom. It's rude and trashy. She's lucky I didn't dump that wine bottle on her head…"

I chuckled. "This is hilarious."

"It's not funny. I don't care that she was hitting on you. I just think that was really rude."

"If you get this upset every time someone is rude, then you must live a bitter life."

She dropped my hand, her attitude flaring up. "How would you feel if some man hit on me while you were in the restroom?"

"That would never happen."

"But what if it did?" she pressed.

"Trust me, it would never happen." No man would be stupid enough to cross me. I terrified any man I came into contact with, and even if they thought Vanessa was their soul mate, they still wouldn't cross that line. I was over two hundred pounds of solid muscle. I was a goddamn beast. Unless the man packed enough ammo for a war, provoking me was a death wish.

"And if it did, would you be upset?"

If a man hit on Vanessa while I went to take a piss, they would be dead. I'd smash their skull into the table until their brains turned into a dish to be served. Not only was she my woman, but the behavior would be disrespectful—and I didn't allow that shit to fly. "Not sure."

She rolled her eyes. "You're so full of shit."

"Admit you're jealous, and I'll reconsider my answer."

"I'm not jealous," she repeated.

"Fine." We arrived at the truck, and I opened the passenger door for her.

She stared at me in surprise. "I didn't know you had manners."

"Don't get used to it." I shut the door behind her and got into the driver's seat. I started the engine, cranked the heat up so Vanessa wouldn't be cold, and then drove back to my apartment.

She stared out the window as we sat in silence.

She shattered the quiet with her gentle words. "Alright…I was jealous."

I grinned even though her words weren't a surprise. "And I'd be even more jealous."

She kept her gaze out the window, not looking at me despite her confession.

I already knew how she felt about me, so admitting this didn't make much of a difference, but seeing her in action was sexy. I liked seeing the rage on her face when she saw me chatting with the brunette when she stepped out into the hallway. She got so mad so fast.

"So...was she hitting on you?"

"Kinda. We slept together before, and she was stopping by to say hi."

Her head snapped in my direction. "You could have kept that information to yourself."

"Why? I don't lie."

"And she wanted to sleep with you again?"

"I think that's where she was going. But I'm not sure. I couldn't even remember her name."

"How could you not remember the name of someone you slept with?" she asked incredulously.

I shrugged. "There's too many to even count...let alone remember."

"You're disgusting." She turned back to the window.

"I'm disgusting?" I asked incredulously. "How many men have you been with?"

"None of your business."

"No, tell me." She thought she could judge me, but I could judge her just as easily.

"I remember all of their names. That's all you need to know."

"Two? Three?"

She refused to answer.

"Come on, baby. You know how to fuck a man, so you have some experience. Four? Five?"

"I didn't ask your number. So why are you asking for mine?"

"Just curious."

"It'll only make you jealous."

I laughed because it was absurd. "I get jealous when men look at you. I get jealous when I think about sharing you. I get jealous if your hand is between your legs instead of me. But I don't get jealous about the men before me. They're all nothing compared to me. I'll wipe away their memory by the time I'm done with you—if I haven't already. They were just practice so you'd be ready for me. Men don't get jealous of boys."

She slowly turned her head back to me, her green eyes reflecting the lights from the dashboard.

I held her gaze for a moment before I turned my eyes back to the road. "You want to know how I got rid of her?"

She didn't ask.

"I told her I was married—and my wife is really jealous."

"Why were you trying to get rid of her? I thought you liked to torture me."

"No." My hand moved to her bare thigh, my fingertips slipping slightly underneath her dress. "Why would I want to be with a woman I don't even remember when I can have the one woman I'll never forget?"

She swallowed the lump in her throat, her eyes on

the road ahead of her. Her thighs tightened together slightly, and her breathing picked up a little. She ran her fingers over her hair. "Drive faster."

"Can't wait to have your way with me, huh?" I asked with a slight grin.

She unbuckled her safety belt then scooted to the middle seat between us. She pressed her body into mine and started kissing my neck and jawline, her hand moving around my chest and to the top of my slacks. "Yes."

I HELD her against my chest in the elevator, her legs wrapped around my waist with her arms locked around my neck. She kissed me with possession as I ground her pussy against my hard dick in my slacks.

Her dress was pulled up to her waist, and her thong was visible in the reflection of the metal doors. I wanted to pin her against the wall and fuck her right then, but I knew I wanted all of her, naked on my bed so I could take my time and enjoy her.

A man could fuck hard, but he should never fuck fast.

The doors opened, and I carried her inside, feeling her want me so desperately her hands shook. She was jealous, possessive, and so deeply attached to me that there was no plausible explanation to make sense of any of this. She hated me, but she wanted me so much she could barely breathe.

Made no goddamn sense.

Maybe she and I would never make sense.

I pulled my kiss away even though she looked heartbroken the second my embrace was gone.

"I left something for you on the bed. Put it on and wait for me. Face down, ass up." Lingerie wasn't a fetish of mine, but I loved having Vanessa put it on obediently and wait for me. It made me feel like I really owned her, had power over her.

She trailed her hands down my chest before she walked away, her hands pulling her dress up over her ass and thong.

I watched her ass shake until she disappeared in the hallway, my cock so hard it nearly burst through my trousers. There was nothing I wanted more than to pull my belt out of the loops and tie her to my headboard. I wanted to take over her body like it was a physical possession. I wanted to restrain her, to teach her that I could give her rights and then take them away.

But I promised her I wouldn't do it again.

I would keep my promise, but I would definitely revisit the conversation.

I poured myself a drink and let the fire move down my throat and into my belly. Picturing her getting dressed, pulling on the teddy and garters, made my cock press harder into my fly. The sexiest woman I'd ever been with was waiting for me, pulling on the lingerie I chose for her so she could be everything I wanted.

Letting her live was the best decision I'd ever made.

Just as I finished the glass, I heard the sound of the elevator.

It hit the bottom floor and then started to move up again.

I wiped my mouth with the back of my forearm and then slowly walked to the system. It was rising because someone had entered the code into the panel.

The code that only I had.

I'd never told it to Max.

And Vanessa didn't know what it was. I made sure she didn't watch me enter the seven-digit pin.

My heart started to pound in my chest because I didn't understand what was going on. It could just be a malfunction of the elevator and wasn't caused by any specific event. Maybe there was nothing wrong at all.

But something told me otherwise.

I hit the button to the camera and saw who was standing inside.

Joe Pedretti and four heavily armed men.

Jesus Christ.

The closest gun I had was in my office, which was at the very end of the hallway. All I had near me was knives from the kitchen. I would run down the hall, but the doors were about to open. If they searched for me, they would find Vanessa.

And I knew exactly what Joe would do with Vanessa.

I'd rather die than let that happen.

The doors opened, and the smug look on Joe's face made my heart fall into my stomach. I didn't know how they'd tracked me down or even figured out it was me, but maybe I'd underestimated them.

And overestimated myself.

I stood with my arms by my sides, refusing to beg or run. I held Joe's gaze without a hint of fear, keeping a stoic expression while I figured out what to do. I was outnumbered, and even if I did have a gun, there wasn't much I could when we were this close to each other.

All four guns were pointed at me.

Joe was the only one who kept his pistol aimed at the ground. "Weren't expecting me?" He spoke with a heavy Italian accent, his arrogance escaping in his tone. He was in a black suit with a black tie, looking like an important man.

But important men didn't need to look important.

"If I were, I would have prepared a nice cheese board and some wine." If this was how I met my end, it wouldn't be on my knees, and it wouldn't be with fear. I'd be the shit-talking asshole I'd always been.

Joe's eyes narrowed in annoyance. "It's easy to pretend when the adrenaline is going. But once the fear replaces it, I don't think you'll be so quick with the jokes."

"It wasn't a joke."

One of his men cocked his gun.

"Ooh…scary," I said sarcastically. "You must mean business."

He smacked the butt of the rifle into my face, making me bleed instantly.

I didn't react at all, not even to wipe the blood away. "That's not how you use a gun, little man."

He clenched his jaw then pointed the barrel right at me. "Then let me show you—"

"Hold on." Joe pressed his gun toward the ground. "I want him on his knees. This is an execution, after all."

I couldn't call for backup, and I couldn't communicate with Vanessa. I hoped they didn't know she was there with me. I suspected they didn't because they would have searched for her the second they walked inside. They were under the impression I was alone. They would kill me then leave—and leave my baby alone.

That was the ideal outcome.

I was about to die, but I wasn't afraid. I knew I would die young. In my line of work, you didn't live long. Something always came up and bit you in the ass. I'd let my emotion cloud my judgment, and now I was about to die without getting the retribution I wanted in the first place.

It was disappointing.

"On your knees." Joe nodded to the ground.

"I prefer to stand," I said sarcastically. "But thanks."

He nodded to his two men.

They came up behind me then kicked both of my legs until I was forced to the ground. Then they tied my wrists together, keeping my hands secured behind my back so I was helpless. My face would crash into the floor the second the bullet was in my brain. I would bleed out all over my apartment.

That's how Vanessa would find me.

Two men remained behind me while the other two kept their guns pointed at me.

Joe placed his gun in his holster. "I've managed to trace you back here. But I haven't figured out your motive. Why did you try to kill me? That has remained a mystery to me."

My eyes caught something in the periphery. Vanessa's form appeared in the hallway, wearing the black lingerie I'd asked her to put on. I didn't look directly at her to give her location away.

I wanted to tell her to hide.

I saw her image disappear a second later, knowing she'd run for it. This was the ideal situation for her. She couldn't pull the trigger herself, but Joe would do the dirty work for her. She wouldn't even have to watch. She would just hear the gunshot, wait for them to leave, and her freedom would be restored.

This would just be a bad dream.

I wished I could say something to her, apologize for the way I'd treated her. She was an innocent person who happened to be the daughter of the man I hated.

She did nothing wrong, and as I got to know her, I recognized all of her wonderful qualities. She didn't deserve what I'd done to her.

I actually felt remorse.

But that didn't matter anymore.

I looked into Joe's face. "You killed my mother."

"Your mother, huh?" he asked. "I kill a lot of people, so you need to be more specific."

"She was a prostitute. It was Christmas Eve. Her name was Lara. She had blond hair and blue eyes. She was beautiful. You fucked her, killed her, and then left her body in a dumpster. I was a small boy at the time, so there was nothing I could do about it. But once I became a man, I decided to punish you for what you did."

"And how did that go?" Joe asked with a laugh. "Now you'll be murdered in your own palace. I wonder how long it will take for someone to realize you're missing…since you don't have anyone."

I felt the pain in my chest but ignored it. Vanessa said something similar to me once, that I only kept up my vendettas because I had nothing else to live for. No family and no friends…I was just alone. I had nothing to lose.

"I don't feel bad for killing your mother. If she didn't want to die, she shouldn't have been a whore."

If those restraints weren't on my wrists, I'd take him down. It would be my last act, and at least I would be doing something productive with it.

"Any last words?" Joe asked.

I snorted until a wad of spit was in my mouth. Then I spat on his shoes. "Fuck off and pull the trigger."

He stared at the top of his shoes, which were now covered in my spit. Anger came on to his face, but instead of telling me off, he nodded to one of his men. "Kill this asshole."

I kept my eyes focused on Joe, knowing the bullet was coming any second. I would die the way I lived, strong and fearless. I was caught with my guard down and that was my fault, but I could still leave this earth with respect and dignity. I hoped Vanessa wasn't watching. I didn't want her to see this. My death would be the best thing for her, but I didn't want it to haunt her for the rest of her life.

The gunshot went off.

Then another.

I closed my eyes, swallowed in darkness. It didn't hurt the way I expected, didn't feel numb either. I'd been shot many times, but not in the head. It didn't feel like anything had happened at all.

Then I heard two bodies fall. One, and then two seconds later, another.

I opened my eyes and saw the commotion around me. Two of the four henchmen were dead, and the others were trying to identify where the shots were coming from.

A bullet hit one of the two in the left eye, sending them crumpling to the ground as their brains flew out the back of their skull. The man standing behind me on my left jerked when a bullet pierced his chest. He fell back, his body landing on the coffee table and shattering the platter that had once belonged to my mother.

Joe was all that was left.

He pulled his pistol out of his harness and aimed.

I pushed my body forward and knocked him over, making him hit the ground and drop the gun.

Vanessa pinned it under her bare foot and kicked it behind her. She stood in the black teddy and garters I'd asked her to wear, looking downright sexy while holding the shotgun in her hands.

Jesus Fucking Christ.

She marched over to Joe and pointed the barrel right in his face. "Move, asshole. I dare you."

He lifted both hands into the air in surrender.

I got to my feet and found a knife in the kitchen. I slit the cable tie in half and let the knife drop to the floor before I walked back to the entryway, seeing Vanessa still standing on top of him.

Joe wasn't nearly as brave as I was. Sweat marked his forehead, and he heaved with his deep breathing. His hands shook, and he pleaded under his breath, his whispers sounding like incoherent phrases.

"Baby, what are you waiting for?" I grabbed Joe's pistol off the ground before I stood over him.

She stepped back and righted her shotgun. "He's all yours." She kept walking back, her bare feet hitting the hardwood floor until she was a safe distance away. "Make him pay for what he did to your mother."

I held the pistol at my side, more entranced by this woman who took down four armed men by herself, headshots to almost all of them, than by my nemesis on the floor. All she'd had to do was keep quiet and hide somewhere, and all of her problems would have disappeared. But she'd risked her life to save me.

The monster who kidnapped her.

Like a wet dream, she killed my enemies in the lingerie I asked her to wear. Her hair was around her shoulders, and her heavy makeup made her eyes dark and lustrous. This was a fantasy I never realized I had.

And it was reality.

I turned back to Joe and raised my gun right at his face.

He put his hands in front of his face. "Look, there's gotta be—"

I shot him in the face twice and once in the chest.

His body went limp, the blood pooling in a puddle on the hardwood floor. His eyes were wide open, and his hands fell to the floor beside him. His suit was ruined, and now he was a dead corpse in the graveyard of his men.

I stared at the face of my enemy, at least, what was left of it. My mother finally avenged, and more importantly, this guy couldn't hurt anyone else. The leader of the Tyrants was killed, along with his top men. I'd killed the rest of them on the street, so hopefully that wiped out most of the organization.

The barrel was empty, so I tossed the gun on the ground, hearing it make a loud thud once the metal clanked against the floor. The silence was somehow louder than the sound of gunshots. It was louder than my frantically beating heart. I'd thought I was going to die just minutes ago, but now I was standing over my enemies.

Because of her.

She set the shotgun on the floor, no longer wanting to touch it now that everyone was dead.

She could have let me die.

She could be free right now.

But she saved me.

I turned to her, speechless for the first time in my life. I didn't know what to say. I was enemies with this woman, and she was enemies with me, but we managed to look the other way in light of the connection that stretched between us.

I could feel that connection now.

She stared at me, her chest rising and falling hard because the adrenaline hadn't passed yet. She didn't have a drop of blood on her, but I had it splashed on my collared shirt.

I unbuttoned it before I let it fall to the floor. Then I moved to her, my eyes set on her just the way they were when she shot me in the snow. She did something so ballsy that I couldn't stop myself from wanting her. She did something that impressed me, and I wasn't the kind of man who was easily impressed.

My hand slid into her hair, and I kissed her in a way I never had before. It slow and sexy, and my arm wrapped around her waist to keep her as close to me as possible. I breathed with her, the adrenaline emerging for a whole different reason entirely. I wasn't scared of anything.

But I was scared of this woman.

I lifted her into my arms and carried her down the hallway, our kissing commencing because nothing was going to slow them down. My cock was so hard in my slacks, so hard it actually hurt. I needed to be buried inside this pussy. Not later after the bodies were dumped. Not after I explained to Max what had happened.

Now.

I dropped her on the bed and pulled her black thong down her gorgeous legs. She worked my slacks, getting them undone so my cock could be free. They weren't pushed all the way down because neither one of us wanted to wait that long.

I parted her legs then sank inside her, my cock sliding through her wetness until I was completely buried within her. I should thank her for what she did, say something about what just happened. But there were no words to describe how I felt about it.

This was the only way I could express myself.

She moaned when she felt all of me, her nails

clawing deep into my back. She grabbed my ass and pulled me deep inside her, breathing against my mouth as she took all of my cock. She rocked back into me, taking my thick length with the same enthusiasm.

My hips thrust over and over, and my body began to slicken in sweat. I wanted to come, but I never wanted this to end. I wanted to stay just like this, my hard cock buried inside this gorgeous pussy. I wanted to be connected like this indefinitely, to share this heat. Nothing else seemed to matter except the two of us.

Because nothing was as important as the two of us.

5

Vanessa

Why did I do it?

I don't have an answer.

I could have let him be executed. It would have fixed my problem without getting my hands dirty. I wouldn't be responsible for his death, and once Joe and his men left, all I had to do was walk out.

And be free.

I would have saved myself.

Saved my family.

But when I watched them put Bones on his knees and bind his wrists, I couldn't take it. I couldn't let this be the end of him. It wasn't fair. He was trying to avenge his mother, and he shouldn't die for protecting his family.

I made my decision without looking back.

I found the shotgun in his office and ran back down the hallway. I'd never handled a shotgun before, only handguns. But I aimed true and hit my mark every time, making their bodies fall to the floor. I took them all out before they even understood what was going on.

The only reason I didn't shoot Joe was because I shouldn't be the one to kill him.

It had to be Bones.

I stepped aside and let him have his revenge. I let him get his closure, let him have the peace he'd been searching for.

And then I let him have me.

He took me to his bed and fucked me all night. He stayed on top of me, giving me all of his big dick as his body got hot and sweaty. Every time he finished, he was ready to go again in a few minutes.

And we kept going.

We didn't exchange a single word. He didn't ask for an explanation, and I didn't give one. We communicated with our bodies, screwing each other's brains out. My pussy overflowed with come because he'd never give me so much before. Every inch of my skin had been kissed by his lips, and by the time we finally went to sleep, my pussy was sore.

He held me in his arms as we slept.

When I woke up the following morning, he was gone.

The bed was empty and cold because he'd been gone for hours. I sat up and searched for him around the room even though I knew he wasn't there. I got out of bed, pulled on a new pair of panties, and grabbed one of his t-shirts. It was way too big for my frame, but it was the most comfortable piece of clothing I'd ever worn.

Because it was his.

After putting on a pair of jeans, I stepped into the hallway and saw him talking with Max in front of the elevator. They were speaking quietly to each other, so I couldn't catch what they were saying. The ground was clean of blood, and the bodies were gone. They shook hands before Max disappeared into the elevator.

Bones stood there even after his friend was gone, his arms crossed over his chest as he stared at the doors to the elevator. He obviously didn't expect his friend to return, but his brain was full of endless thoughts.

I emerged from the hallway, stepping out exactly the way I did last night—when I killed all those men.

He turned to me, dressed in his gray sweatpants without a shirt. Ink covered his skin everywhere, the black color weaving endless stories across his muscled physique. He watched me with a stoic expression, hiding his thoughts from me as best he could.

I knew everything was different now.

I crossed a line I couldn't uncross, and now we had to discuss what that meant.

Bones had to end the blood war against my family. He owed me.

And he knew it.

He dropped his arms then approached me, his broad shoulders powerful and the look in his eyes gentle. His hands moved to my waist, and he kissed me, a soft kiss that was just lips. He pulled me tighter into him, and my tits pressed against his body.

Whenever I was with this man, everything about my life faded away. All I knew was I wanted more of him, more of this feeling he gave me. He made me feel safe, and if he were ever in danger, I wouldn't think twice before helping him. I needed him to be alive. I needed him to be safe. I shouldn't care whether he lived or died, but I cared from the bottom of my heart. "You got rid of them…?" My arms circled his waist, and I rested my face against his chest.

"Yes."

"How?"

"Max helped me dispose of them. We dropped them in Lake Garda."

"You've been awake for a long time, then."

"I never went to sleep." His hand moved under the fall of my hair, and he rested his chin on my forehead.

"Do we have to worry about the rest of his men?"

"Unlikely. All they'll care about is who will replace him, not who will avenge him. Besides, they'll be afraid of me now."

"Do you feel better…now that he's gone?"

He stepped back so he could look into my face. "I do." He rested his forehead against mine and closed his eyes. "Because of you."

WE SAT across from each other at the kitchen table, our plates empty because we'd finished our dinner. Bones didn't eat much and spent most of his time drinking his scotch. I sipped my wine, not in the mood for a big dinner either.

Bones stared at me across the table, his fingers resting on the rim of his glass. Sometimes he spun his fingers around the edge, his callused tips rubbing across the surface. He'd already had two glasses, so now he seemed to be pacing himself by purposely slowing down.

I stared at the beautiful man across from me, knowing he deliberately wasn't speaking. We both knew I could have turned my cheek and let him be executed in his entryway. I could have hidden away and waited until his murder was finished. If I hadn't picked up that shotgun, we wouldn't be sitting here right now.

That meant the relationship had changed.

But how much did it change?

Bones downed the rest of his glass before he set it down. He licked his lips then rested his forearms on the table, the corded veins protruding from his tight skin. His muscles were thick and veined, and he was a beefy man who seemed too heavy to sit in his chair. "You could have let me die." He finally started the conversation, got the ball rolling.

"I know."

"You could have hidden until they left."

"I know…"

"But you didn't. And I don't understand why." He didn't look down once, holding my gaze with his ice-blue expression. He showed his affection all night and morning, but now we couldn't pretend there hadn't been a major shift underneath our feet. Like an earth-quake had struck, the ground was cracked and broken, and now the foundation had been completely destroyed.

What was left?

"Why?" he repeated.

I didn't have a concrete answer, and there hadn't been much thinking that went on. It was all instinct. I only had seconds to make up my mind and intervene. If I'd sat there and tried to decide what I should do, he would have been killed. "I couldn't let you die. It's that simple."

"But my death would have fixed all your problems."

"I'm aware…" I could be back in my apartment right now, the shackles free from my ankles and wrists. My family would be safe. Bones was my tormentor, and he kept me as his prisoner for two months. All I had to do was nothing. "But I just…" I looked away, unable to meet his gaze.

"Look at me."

I refused.

"Baby." His tone was hard and soft at the same time.

I breathed a sigh before I shifted my gaze back to him.

"Just what?" he whispered.

"You've done horrible things to me. You aren't a good man. You've threatened to kill my family multiple times…but you're such a big part of my life now. You're the man I'm sleeping with, the man I get jealous over, and the man who makes me feel safe at night. There's two different versions of you. There's the one I hate… and there's the other one. If I let you die, both of you die."

He remained absolutely still, motionless like a statue.

"You're right, I could have let you die. No one would have judged me for it. But it's because of me that you were able to get revenge for your mother. You were able to put that vendetta to rest so you can move on with your life. Now you owe me." I swallowed the emotion in my voice and found my strength to remain strong. "You owe me for saving your life. And you owe me for giving Joe to you."

"They're one and the same," he whispered.

"What does it matter?"

"Because I owe you for one thing, not two." He rested his fingers over his empty glass. "And you're right. I do owe you. I'm an honest man who honors my debts. You saved me when you didn't have to, and I—"

"Spare my family." I knew exactly what I wanted. I wanted my family to be safe from his wrath. I wanted them to continue their peaceful lives. They were so happy and had so much to be thankful for. If Bones threatened them, all the peace they worked for would be destroyed. "That's what I want. Nothing else."

His chest rose and fell heavily with the deep breath he took. "You know I can't do that…"

My jaw almost dropped. "Are you fucking kidding me? I could have let you die—"

"I know. But you need to understand that your parents took everything from me—"

"Your father took everything from you because he was a psychotic rapist. He kidnapped my aunt, raped her, and then he killed her right in front of my father. And then he raped my mother, who's the best woman on this planet, and my father didn't just let the past repeat itself. He did something about it and saved her. If you're going to sit there and act like your father is the victim in all this—"

He raised his hand to silence me. "Baby, I understand—"

"Don't fucking 'baby' me," I hissed. "Leave my family alone. I saved your life so you could get revenge for your mother. You owe me, asshole. You fucking owe me. If your father wasn't such a piece of shit, he would be alive right now. He wasn't a good man, and we both know it. So shut up about it."

His face remained stoic, and he didn't get angry like he usually would. "I've heard you—loud and clear."

"Then you're a psychopath just like your father." I crossed my arms over my chest so I wouldn't smash the bottle over his skull. Now I really did want to him kill him.

"I have something else to offer you," he said calmly.

"There's nothing I want more than my family's safety. That's all I want—nothing else."

"What about you?"

"What about me?" I countered. "What does that even mean?"

"You saved my life, and now I'll spare yours. We're even. I promise I'll never hurt you, Vanessa. I'll never lay a hand on you. I'll never try to kill you. Regardless of how I feel about your family, you're safe."

I stopped breathing because the offer was tempting. I was always scared that he might change his mind and send me to the guillotine. Every day was a gift because he could take it away. But now I wouldn't have to live with that fear anymore.

"And you're also free."

"Free?"

"You aren't my prisoner anymore. You can do whatever you want. I don't own you anymore."

My life would be mine again.

"And then we're even," he said. "You have my word I'll never go back on it."

This man made me feel equally safe and equally scared, but now there was no reason to be afraid.

"You will always have my protection. If you need anything, I'll be there for you. I'll lay down my life to save yours. I'm committed for life. That's what I offer you, baby. Your life and your freedom. I think that's more than fair."

The original arrangement was my servitude in exchange for my family's safety. But now that that was off the table, what did that mean for them? "Then you're going to kill them tomorrow? Next week? My freedom means nothing if I'm about to lose everyone I love."

He held my gaze, his look cold.

I was so frustrated, I was on the verge of tears. I tried to see the good in this man, but I was starting to realize there was none. He was blinded by his hate, condemned to suffer forever because he didn't know how else to live. It didn't matter how much I gave him, he would never appreciate it. I closed my eyes for a brief moment, and two tears started to run down my cheeks. "I don't understand you. I've given you everything. I've spared your life many times. But that's never enough for you. There's more to you than this blood lust. There's more to you than all this hate. I know there is…"

His eyes shifted down. "There's not, Vanessa. I'm sorry I misled you."

"You didn't mislead me. You're misleading yourself."

His eyes moved up again.

"I wish I'd let you die. I wish…" More tears came. "It doesn't matter what I wish." I rose from the chair and walked to the entryway. I'd left my phone and belongings behind, but I didn't care. He could keep my paintings, keep my phone and wallet and everything else I owned.

It meant nothing to me anymore.

"Where are you going?" he asked, not rising from his seat.

I didn't turn around before I got inside the elevator. "You said I was free. It's none of your damn business where I'm going." I hit the button and forced the doors to close so I wouldn't have to look at him ever again.

Once the doors were shut and I had my privacy, I let the tears out. I thought this man had more inside that hollow chest, but now I knew he was as evil as he'd always claimed. I couldn't stop him. Even saving his life wouldn't change his mind.

By the time I reached the ground, I was sobbing. "Why didn't I kill him?"

My father would be so disappointed in me.

My whole family would be.

If they all died and I lived…I wouldn't be able to live with that regret.

I would kill myself.

I stepped out into the cold night air, wearing a t-shirt and jeans. The icy temperature felt good against my hot face. It was a windy night, so my hair flapped around me and my tears were flung onto the concrete. I crossed my arms over my chest and stepped forward, ready to brave the cold evening air on my way to…wherever.

I didn't even have my keys.

I felt a shadow move on top of me, and I knew I was standing underneath a mountain. His chest came into view, and I refused to look at his eyes.

His evil eyes.

I stepped around him. "Leave me alone."

He grabbed me by the elbow. "Vanessa."

I twisted out of his grasp. "Don't touch me again. If I'm free, you'll let me go. I never want to look at your face again. I never want to hear you speak. I want nothing to do with you. Go back inside, put a gun in your mouth, and pull the damn trigger." I moved forward again, feeling no regret for what I'd just said.

Only for what I hadn't done.

He moved into my path again. "Wait. I'll drop it."

"Drop what?"

"I'll leave your family alone."

It was too good to be true. I lifted my gaze and met his eyes, seeing the sincerity in his face. "You promise?"

"I promise I'll drop it…for now."

"For now? What does that mean?"

"It means I'll drop the vendetta for the foreseeable future."

"Until when?"

"I don't know. But that's the best I can give you."

It was hard to see his face because my hair was flapping so hard in the wind. "That's not enough, Bones. Not even close."

"Then let me think about it. I won't do anything

until I've made a decision, and I'll genuinely consider what you said…and you can convince me why I should drop this blood war. That's the best you're going to get out of me, and I honestly think it's more than fair."

"Am I still free?"

He nodded. "You're always free. You're always safe."

If that was the best I was going to get, then I would just accept it and appreciate it. My family was safe for now, and I had time to change his mind. I managed to get him to reconsider, and that was significant progress for a bitter man like him.

"Come back inside." He scooped his arms underneath me and carried me back into the building.

I didn't fight him because I didn't want to be out there anyway. The second I was against his warm chest, I felt safe from the wind. I felt safe from everything—even him. My arms hooked around his neck, and I rode with him in the elevator, thinking about the last time we were inside, of the way we kissed and touched. I was attached to this man more than I'd ever been to anyone else.

But I knew he was attached to me too—and that gave me hope.

I WOKE up the next morning with his face close to mine. His heavy arm was around my waist, and my leg was hooked over his waist. His eyes were open, like he'd been watching me for a while.

My eyes blinked a few times before the image in front of me became clearer. I took in his beautiful eyes, his muscled frame, and the scruff that formed along his jaw. I was a free woman, and I didn't have to be there anymore—but there I was.

We didn't screw last night. He carried me to bed, and we went to sleep. I wasn't sure how I felt about him anymore. I was angry that he wouldn't give me what I wanted, but I appreciated the fact that he gave me something.

My freedom.

And a chance to convince him to move on from his blood lust.

I'd been sleeping with him for over two months now, so I wasn't sure what else I could do to convince him he needed to spare my family. I was kind to him, and instead of letting him die, I did something about it.

Wasn't that enough?

He didn't say a word as he watched me, his bright blue eyes watching my gaze without blinking. I was used to his stare, but this one felt different somehow. It felt warm instead of cold. It felt affectionate rather than invasive.

Now that I had this newfound freedom, I wasn't sure what to do with it. Regardless of what decisions I made, my life was spared. He vowed never to hurt me or to lay a hand on me. I could reclaim some of my life, the life I'd been missing.

I pulled back the sheets and got out of bed.

Bones sat up and watched me.

I didn't pull on his t-shirt the way I usually would. After waking up, we usually had morning sex, then I would go into my art room and he would head to his office. But that routine was over, starting today.

I pulled on a pair of jeans and a long-sleeved shirt before I started to pack my bag.

Bones got out bed then stood behind me. "You're leaving."

I didn't look at him, concentrating on pulling my clothes out of the drawer and placing them inside my bag. I could feel his piercing gaze right between my shoulder blades, like he was holding a branding iron against me. "I'm free to do whatever I want, right?"

He was quiet for an eternity, like he might not say anything at all. He'd granted me my freedom, but he obviously struggled to keep his word. He wanted to grab me by the arm and yank me onto the bed. He wanted to do what we did every morning, not caring if I wanted the same thing. But now, everything was different. I could feel the struggle right behind me, feel him clench his fists in frustration. "Yes."

"Then I want to go home." I zipped up my bag and then walked down the hall to the art room. I was taking my paintings with me, so I grabbed the paper and started to cover each one, to protect them from sunshine, humidity, and the pollutants in the air.

He stood in the doorway and watched me. "Does that mean you aren't coming back?" He crossed his arms over his muscled chest, his ink stretching down both arms and up his corded neck.

"I don't know." I had no idea what I was doing at this point. I just knew I needed some space. "I think I'm going down south to spend time with my family. I want to put up my artwork at the winery anyway. Might be good for me to have a change of scenery…"

"Are you going to tell them?"

I knew exactly what he was asking—if I was going to tell them everything about him. If I did, my family would immediately mobilize and prepare to bury him six feet under. I could start the war and give them the upper hand. "No. And that's only because I believe you'll make the right decision."

"You need to stop seeing the good in others—when it's not there."

"There's good in you, Bones. It's just buried so far down that you can't see it." I finished wrapping all the paintings then set them on the floor. "If you do decide you're going to move forward with it, I want to know first."

He continued to lean against the doorframe.

"I want to warn them what's coming. But I'll be on the other side of the battlefield—and this time, I will kill you."

His expression didn't change, but I knew he was fighting to keep his face neutral.

I meant what I said. If he made me choose between him and my family, I would choose my family. I didn't have the strength to kill him when it was just the two of us, but if my parents' lives were on the line, I'd shoot him right between the eyes.

I knew it in my heart.

I picked up two paintings and then moved toward the door even though his massive frame was blocking it. "Will you do that for me?"

He cocked his head to the side slightly, examining me with those pretty eyes. "Alright."

"Promise?"

He gave a slight nod. "Promise." He stepped out of the way to let me pass.

"Can you give me a ride home?" I didn't have a car or a way to transport all of my things. I moved into the hallway and turned around when I didn't hear him follow me.

He remained in front of the doorway, pressing his hands against the frame. All the muscles of his torso tightened, his displeasure obvious. He fought the urge to say no, fought the urge to tie me up and keep me there forever. He clenched his jaw before he answered, his words coming out restrained. "Yes."

HE HELPED me carry all of my things into the apartment. My place wasn't ideal to house all of my paintings. We leaned them up against the wall in the living room, the images taking up all the available space in the area. There was hardly room for my easel. Thankfully, they wouldn't be there for long since I would drop them off with my parents.

I set my bag on the couch then looked at him, feeling the tension increase between us. The silence was deafening, nearly bursting my eardrums because it was so loud. Goose bumps formed on my arms, and the hair on the back of my neck was standing up. All my emotions were contradictory because I wanted him to stay, but I also couldn't wait for him to leave.

He stood by the door, his arms crossed and his t-shirt stretched. His jeans hung low on his hips, and since he hadn't shaved for a few days, his jaw was sprinkled with masculine scruff. I liked the way it felt between my legs when his mouth was pressed to my most tender areas.

I'd never seen a more beautiful man all my life. I'd never been so passionate with someone, needed someone the way I needed him. It was the only way to explain my behavior, my impulse to save his life. If he didn't mean anything to me, I would have looked the other way and let it happen. But something told me I would be devastated if I lost this man.

But knowing my actions weren't enough to spare my family made me resent him, even if he said he would consider ending the war. I was relieved I was free, but just because he gave me permission to do what I wanted didn't necessarily mean I was free from this man… because I could still feel the connection between us. It was overwhelming and powerful.

"When are you leaving?" He broke the silence with his masculine voice, his deep and reverberating baritone vibrating his throat.

"Tomorrow."

"How long will you be gone?"

"I'm not sure…probably a week."

His eyes showed his disappointment, but he didn't voice it. "Can I stay with you?"

I'd never heard him ask for anything since the day I met him. There was no such thing as him asking for permission. He just took what he wanted—and everyone else had to accept it. I could feel the anger in his voice when he asked the question because it was so difficult for him to do. He still felt like he owned me even after he'd set me free. "No. I just want some space right now." I'd spent every waking hour with this man, and I needed some time alone. After all this time, I thought I understood him, but I realized I didn't understand him at all.

He clenched his jaw hard but didn't give in to the rage inside his chest. He gave me a slight nod. "Call me if you need anything."

"Alright." I was surprised he was actually going to

listen to me. I assumed he would storm across the room and kiss me until he got what he wanted.

"I mean it. Anything at all."

"I know…"

He gave me a long look before he turned around and left my apartment.

He actually left.

I really did have my freedom back, my independence. I thought it would give me a high, give me a sense of power.

But his absence only made me feel alone.

———

I CLEANED MY APARTMENT, ordered a pizza, and then occupied myself by watching TV while lying on the couch. It was the first time I'd been alone since I got into trouble with Bones in the first place. Now I could do whatever I wanted, even go out and meet a guy. I still had the tracker in my ankle, but even if he was watching my whereabouts, there was nothing he could do about it.

When it started to get late, I went into my bedroom and got under the covers. I cranked up the heater a little higher than I usually did because it was too cold. Bones's body had provided an extra ten degrees of warmth. He heated the sheets and kept me comfortable all night long.

It was the first time I went to bed in a sweater.

Now I wasn't used to my own bed anymore—not without him.

Every time I closed my eyes and tried to drift off to sleep, I heard a noise. It was pop here or a crack somewhere else. My paranoid mind got the best of me, and I kept walking into the living room to explore the sound.

I peeked out my window and saw nothing there. I checked the windows and made sure the front door was locked. Knuckles had broken in to my apartment, and now I'd seen five men break in to Bones's place despite all of his security measures.

I didn't feel safe anymore.

I went back to bed, but then the apartment would make strange noises, so I would get up again and check over and over.

I was used to his deep breathing drowning out all other sounds, and I was used to staying at his place more often than staying at mine. And I was used to knowing he would handle anything that came our way. I didn't have to care about the strange noises because I had a bulletproof man to protect me.

I'd seen him be shot twice—and both times, it didn't affect him.

How was that possible?

I kept getting up and checking the apartment, afraid that someone was watching me now that Bones was gone.

But I never saw anything.

I was just being paranoid.

I went back to bed and saw the time on the clock on my nightstand.

It was two in the morning.

Damn, I wasn't going to get any sleep tonight.

I grabbed my phone and held it on my stomach, tempted to call the man I'd asked to leave me alone. I would judge myself if I turned to him, would loathe myself if I asked him to protect me. He was my biggest enemy.

But once the next sound erupted, I called him.

It barely rang one time before he answered. "Baby."

I listened to the silence over the phone, hoping to catch the sound of his breathing. But I couldn't discern any noise. I imagined he was lying in bed. He obviously wasn't asleep because he didn't sound like he'd just woken up.

I loathed myself for making the call, but the second I heard his voice, I felt better. I felt like his presence could keep the demons outside my apartment.

He didn't ask why I called. He just sat there with me, listening to me breathe.

I could stay like that forever.

What was wrong with me?

He spoke after five minutes of silence. "Are you alright?"

No, I wasn't alright. I was so fucked up in the head I didn't know what to do with myself. I missed a man I despised. I saved a man I should have killed. "I can't sleep. I keep hearing all these noises, and it's scaring me…" I hated admitting I was scared. I hated admitting any kind of weakness, especially to him. I was bred to be as strong as my brother, as strong as my mother.

"It's nothing," he whispered. "Go to sleep."

"How do you know it's nothing?"

No answer.

My heart started to beat a little faster as I considered what he'd said. He was a paranoid man, overly protective. For him to brush off my concern was unlike him. Unless he knew something I didn't. "You're outside, aren't you?"

No answer.

I wondered how long he'd been out there.

"I'm sitting in my truck at the curb. I haven't seen anyone all night."

I sat up in bed and leaned against the headboard, my heart beating a little faster. "Why?"

"You know why."

"But I want to hear you say it."

He sighed into the phone. "I worry about you, baby. You're sleeping in there by yourself, and it scares me. Knuckles got you once, and then Joe's men could have gotten you a second time. At least, if I'm here, I know that can't happen again."

I closed my eyes, feeling my heart slow down until it turned into a dull ache. It shouldn't mean anything to me that he was out there in the cold. I shouldn't want to invite him inside. I shouldn't have called him in the first place.

"So you can sleep now. I'll be out here until morning."

"And when will you sleep?"

"After you get to your parents' place."

All I had to do was hang up and go to sleep. But I stayed on the phone, struggling with the words that wanted to burst out of my throat.

When he knew I wouldn't say anything else, he ended the call. "Good night, baby."

"Wait…"

"It's okay. You said you wanted space. I'm not out here hoping for an invitation."

"But I'm giving you an invitation—and I know you can't say no."

He was quiet for a long time, his breathing increasing slightly. I heard the door to his truck open and then the click of the phone as the line went dead.

He was coming.

I heard the front door open and close and then heard his heavy footsteps against the hardwood floor. His shadowed figure appeared in the doorway, six-foot-three of muscle and strength. His outline was intimidating, even to me when I knew he would never hurt me, not after he promised he wouldn't.

I knew I would be able to sleep well for the rest of the night.

He stripped down to his boxers then crawled into bed beside me. The mattress dipped with his weight, and then his smell surrounded me. He lay still next to me, not touching me like he normally would. His head rested on the pillow, and he stared at me, stared at me exactly the same way he had that morning. "No one can ever get to you as long as I'm here. So sleep."

I moved into his chest and hooked my leg over his waist and my arm around his torso. My face was pressed close to his, and I could feel his gentle breaths from his nose. We shared one pillow and one side of the bed because we were so close together. I could feel his hard dick in his boxers, but I knew an advance wasn't coming.

My eyes felt heavy as the exhaustion suddenly hit me hard. I'd been scared of every noise that echoed through the house, and now all the sounds died away because they didn't matter. I didn't feel alone or unprotected.

I felt like nothing in the world could ever hurt me.

This man was bulletproof.

And he would protect me with his life, whether someone was after me or not.

My eyes were closed, but I could feel his gaze on my face. I could feel his piercing stare with those pretty blue eyes. I could feel his strong pulse under my fingertips, feel his hard dick against my clit.

I fell asleep almost instantly, feeling safe with a monster.

BONES CARRIED all my luggage to the car and arranged my paintings in the back seat so they would all fit. He did all of this without me asking him to, being a gentleman when he was nothing of the sort.

He walked me to the car in the parking lot, dressed in the clothes he'd been wearing the night before. He didn't seem tired even though he'd spent most of his evening in a freezing-cold truck. He was in his black hoodie and black jeans, the dark color contrasting against his fair skin. He was a much lighter color than I was, skin the color of milk, his eyes the color of glaciers, and his hair dirty-blond.

We didn't have sex last night or this morning. He didn't try anything, and I didn't initiate it either. We'd had the best sex we'd ever had after I killed those men. Bones didn't bother cleaning up the bodies because he cared more about having me. We did it nonstop in his bedroom, and only when the sun came up did we finally go to sleep.

But that was the last time.

Now there was this distance between us.

I was a free woman. How did I want to enjoy my freedom?

He leaned against the trunk of the car, his body making the car shift slightly under his weight. He stared at me with little expression, his emotions not readable in his eyes. He stared at me for a moment before he turned his gaze to the ground. "You can always call me. Doesn't matter what time it is."

"I know. What are you going to do?"

"Not sure yet. I might take a job."

"Well, be safe if you do."

The corner of his mouth rose in a smile, but it didn't last long before it came down a second later. "Yeah...I will."

"Well, goodbye." I'd never said that word to him, but now I didn't know if this would be the last time we spoke. I didn't know what we were. I didn't know what lay ahead for us. Even if he said he would spare my family, would we still have a relationship? I'd like to think we wouldn't, but I was the one who called him last night.

He turned his gaze to me, the hurt in his eyes. He didn't hide that expression from me this time. He either couldn't control it, or he didn't want to. He clenched his jaw for a moment before he straightened, removing his weight from the car. Without saying a word, he walked away. His powerful body shifted and moved as he walked, and he carried himself like a man who hadn't been shot and stabbed so many times. Nothing could defeat him.

Not even me.

"THESE ARE SO BEAUTIFUL." Mom unwrapped each one and hung them on the wall at the winery, placing them on the white background so the color could really stand out. The tables and chairs were in the center of the room, where customers gathered to enjoy their wine and cheese while they had a breathtaking view of the winery. "I love them all."

"Thanks, Mom." I hooked one onto the wall, feeling the back of it catch the string.

She bent down to open another and then carefully removed the brown paper that protected it against the elements. Instead of hanging it up, she held it in her hands for a long time and stared at it.

She stared at it for a long time.

I had ten different pieces that I'd been working for the past month, so I wasn't sure which one she was looking at or why she liked it so much.

"Who is this?" Her smile was gone, and her bubbly attitude had disappeared. She was so happy just a moment ago, but now she was deathly serious.

"Who?" I asked.

She moved toward me so I could see the image. "This man."

I stared at the painting, sick to my stomach when I realized I'd packed it by mistake. I meant to leave that at home in the other room, but I must have gotten it mixed up with a different image.

Mom kept staring at it, looking at the snowy background. The snow traveled all the way to the water and to the small dock that stretched across the flat lake. The trees surrounding the area were all dead, just twigs that reached up into the sky.

Bones stood with his back to the viewer, his muscled frame and immense body obvious in the black sweater and jeans he wore. Vapor escaped his mouth as he stared at the lake. He'd just finished dumping the man into the water, and now he admired the scenery before him, the solitude he thrived on. He was mysterious at the time, a man who terrified me but aroused me simultaneously. It was the first time I'd kissed him, that night in the snow.

And it was a kiss I'd never forget.

I shot him in the shoulder, but that didn't slow him down.

Nothing could slow him down, not when I was the target he was trying to reach.

I tried to find an explanation, to think of something to explain the odd image. All of my other paintings were just landscapes in Milan. Only people I knew well had appearances in my pieces, people I could paint because I knew their features like the back of my hand.

It was the painting I hadn't wanted Bones to see. I didn't want him to understand how I saw him. On that night, he was a murderer and a monster. But instead of seeing the blood on his hands and the violence in his eyes, I saw him as misunderstood.

He was a man in pain.

A man who was lost.

I finally found my voice. "No one. I'd never painted a lake before, and I wanted to give it a try… I was never planning on selling it. I must have put it in the car by accident."

Mom kept holding it and refused to let go. "Why wouldn't you sell it? It's your best work." She finally pulled her gaze away and looked at me. She didn't ask the question that was burning in her eyes, but the look on her face told me what she was thinking.

He wasn't no one.

She moved to a free spot on the wall and hooked the string on the nail before she let it hang. "It's different from all of your other pieces, much moodier…and emotional. I can see it in the colors. I can see it in the way this man is standing. I love all of your work, but this one is particularly beautiful."

"Thanks…"

"Lake Garda, right?"

I nodded. "Yeah."

"What should the price be?" she asked. "Most of your pieces are three thousand euros. This one should be at least four." She grabbed the blank business card and wrote the price on the back with her pretty handwriting. Then she placed it next to the picture.

I should just get rid of it. I shouldn't keep any memory of that man. He would become a memory I would try to forget. But the idea of someone putting it up in their house, staring at one of my most emotional memories, didn't sit right with me. I wanted it to myself. I wanted to hang it in my bedroom. He had a painting to remember me.

I wanted one to remember him.

"It's...it's not for sale." I took it off the wall and wrapped it in the paper again, making sure my father wouldn't see it. My father was just as intuitive as my mother, and it was difficult to hide things from him. I opened the closet and placed it inside so no one would take it by accident. I shut the door again then faced my mother.

Her eyes were filled with emotion, filled with that perceptive look I'd been getting all my life.

She knew.

THE FOLLOWING THREE days passed quickly.

It was nice to spend time with my family. It'd been a while since it was just the three of us. When Conway moved out, it was the three of us for a long time. When it was my turn to leave the nest, it was difficult for my parents to let me go.

Even though they put on a brave face.

Now we spent all our time together, working at the winery during the day and having long dinners in the evening. There weren't many wine tastings going on in the winter, but people still stopped by, mainly locals looking for something to do.

My mother never mentioned the painting.

But I knew it was only a matter of time.

I didn't contact Bones, and he didn't contact me.

He gave me the space I asked for, even though it killed him to do it. When he walked away from me, I knew it was difficult for him to turn his back. He probably stared at his phone every night wondering if I would call.

He probably thought about calling me but changed his mind before his finger could hit the send button.

On the fourth day, it rained, so my family and I stayed home. Father worked in his office on the third floor, and Mom and I made cookies in the kitchen. We used to do it when I was little, and since Lars wasn't in the kitchen as much as he used to be, we didn't have to fight him for the territory.

"How's Lars doing?" I asked as I placed the dry ingredients in a bowl.

"Good." Mom used the mixer to gently stir the sugar with the butter, getting it combined evenly so the cookies would be spectacular. Both of us hardly ate sweets, so when we made them, it was more for the busywork than the actual reward. "He's been taking it easy. He relaxes a lot more than he used to, which makes your father and me happy. We've urged him to retire and just relax, but he insists on working until the day he dies."

"Talk about commitment…"

Mom chuckled. "He just loves this job and this house. But we told him he's welcome to live here even if he stops working. A retirement package for him."

"And he still said no?" I asked incredulously.

She shrugged. "Italian men are very stubborn. You know that."

Bones popped into my head, and I couldn't agree more. He was more stubborn than I was...and that was quite an accomplishment. "All too well."

We continued preparing the dough before we started to scoop them onto the pan. We divided them evenly before we set them in the oven.

"It's been really nice having you around the house again." Mom took off her oven mitts and set them on the counter. "Just like how it used to be before you left for school." She grabbed an open bottle of wine from the fridge and poured two glasses.

"Do you guys ever drink water?"

She drank from her glass before she set it down. "Do you?"

I grinned. "Touché, Mama." I took a long drink, feeling the smooth flavor all the way down.

She pulled out a fresh baguette and some cheese, and we stood at the kitchen counter as we snacked and drank wine. The cookies would only be ten minutes, so it didn't seem like enough time to get comfortable at the dining table. "I haven't seen your father drink water since I first met him. He sticks to scotch. Wine is water to him."

"If I have more than two glasses of wine, I'm already tipsy. Another glass and I would be drunk. No idea how he does it."

"He has a very high tolerance, I guess."

"Or maybe he's drunk all the time," I said with a laugh.

"If that's the case, I'm very impressed. And I wonder what he's like sober."

"Can't even imagine."

She finished her wine and then refilled her glass. "So…" When she paused after the word, I knew something was coming. She didn't start sentences like that unless the subject matter was delicate.

She was going to ask about the man in the painting.

"Your father is really good friends with Pierre, the owner of La Chalet in Milan."

Not at all what I was expecting. "Oh?" I grabbed another piece of bread and smeared the cheese across the surface.

"And he mentioned he saw you there the other night…with a very handsome man."

Shit. Why did he have to take me to that fancy place in Milan? Dinner at some random café would have been perfectly fine. I should have known I would be recognized. Any place that served Barsetti wine should have been off-limits. Now I felt my mother stare at me hard, her blue eyes calculating.

She sipped her wine but didn't say anything more, letting the silence suffocate the conversation.

I had to say something, but I didn't know what. I was usually quick with rebuttals, but when it came to Bones, I didn't have the same strength I used to. He made me more confused than I'd ever felt in my life.

"He also mentioned he was a big guy...very muscular."

Like in the painting. Shit. Why did my mother have to be so damn smart?

"Sweetheart, you know I never pry into your personal life. At least, I try not to. But I've never needed to because we've always talked about these sorts of things. From your first crush to your first kiss...we've always had a pretty open relationship. And I love that about us. And now...I feel like you're keeping me in the dark on purpose."

Because I was. I was keeping everyone in the dark. He was my dirty secret. But I could never come clean to my mother, not when it was a conflict of interest. Bones was an enemy to our family, and if I mentioned anything to her, the war would begin. If I kept my mouth shut and worked with Bones a little longer, maybe I could end it for good. "I don't want to talk about it." I drank from my glass and saw the hurt look stretch across my mother's face. It made me feel like the worst daughter on the planet.

"Can I ask why?"

"I just...I don't want to." I couldn't think of a better reason than the blunt truth.

"Because it seems like this is a pretty intense and deep relationship."

My eyes flicked back to hers. "What makes you say that?" She didn't even know it was Bones, so how would she know that?

"That painting says it all, sweetheart."

It was just an image of him looking out into the water. It didn't even show his face. How could she deduce that? "I don't know what you mean…"

"I can feel so much emotion from that painting. That man is a major component in your life now. I've never seen you paint anyone but your family. But you took the time to paint him…because he means a lot to you."

He didn't mean anything to me. He was just a man who had turned my life upside down.

"Your father has been a lot better about you growing up and being a grown woman. I think the space and distance have helped him understand that you're a woman who's old enough to have those kinds of relationships. So, if you're afraid of him—"

"I'm not. He told me if I ever wanted to introduce him to a man, he would like to meet him."

"Then what is the problem?"

"Well, Father made it clear he only wanted to meet the man that would be my husband…"

"And?"

I stared down into my glass. "This man will never be my husband." Bones wasn't even my boyfriend. He was a man I'd become attached to for many horrible reasons. I used him to feel safe. I used him for good sex. Now he was such a big part of my life, it was hard to imagine not having him there. It was hard to sleep without his large body right next to me.

"Why are you so sure of that?"

"I just am." I finished my wine and immediately grabbed the bottle to pour another glass.

She tilted her head slightly, trying to think of the right thing to say. "When I met your father, I didn't think he'd ever be my husband either."

She'd never told me about the beginning of their relationship, but now I knew he'd rescued her from Bones's father. Bones claimed my father took my mother for his own revenge. I didn't want to believe it because my father was such a good man, it was hard to imagine him doing anything other than worshiping the ground my mother walked on. "Then what did you think?"

"I thought...we would go our separate ways eventually. He wasn't my type. He was dark, cold, insufferable at times... He wouldn't open up to me, no matter how many times I asked him to. Our physical relationship deepened over the course of a year, but he did his best to keep his emotions out of the situation. In that amount of time, I'd come to accept your father for what he was—and even love him for it. It took him a while to reciprocate, but once it happened, the rest of our lives have been exactly the same. Our bond is strong, our loyalty to one another is stronger. I love him more now than I did when I met him thirty years ago."

It sounded so similar to my relationship with Bones that my hand shook a little.

"What I'm trying to say is, when we're young, we

imagine our future husband. He's always a knight in shining armor. He's always on a white horse. He's always Prince Charming. So when we meet a man who doesn't fit that description, we assume he's wrong for us. But there are good men out there, even if they don't seem that way at first. Sometimes it takes a while to see the goodness underneath. I've learned that love is about accepting your partner and loving him not in spite his flaws, but *because* of them."

"I don't love him," I blurted. I said it so harshly that I didn't recognize my own voice. I gnashed my teeth together, wanting those words to sound as true as possible. My connection to him was based on physical lust and intimacy. I only saved his life because I hoped he was a better man than he seemed. I could never love a man who despised my family, who despised the people I loved most in this world.

She stared at me with the same expression my father sometimes wore, like she could see right through me. It was a ghostly expression, pregnant with supernatural powers. "If you want him to believe that, don't show him that painting."

6

Bones

Five days came and went, and I didn't hear from Vanessa.

I watched her tracker almost constantly, but she never deviated from two locations—her childhood home and the winery.

The last time we spoke, there was a hint of finality to the conversation. She said goodbye to me, like she wanted it to be the last time she ever saw me. I brushed it off and walked away.

She'd call.

Right now, she felt comfortable with her parents. But the second she was back home, I would be the first person she called. She wanted to push me away, but we were both too invested in this.

Our relationship was obviously different now, and I wasn't sure what was going to happen. I wasn't even sure what we were anymore. She was a free woman now. I had absolutely no power over her.

And I'd put the war on hold—for her.

So where did that leave us?

I was a man with needs, and if she wasn't fulfilling those needs, I would go elsewhere. She wasn't calling me either. If she was going to drop me like that, I would do the same thing to her.

I went out that night, hitting up a bar with Max.

He sat beside me at the bar in a long-sleeved black t-shirt. His third bottled beer sat in front of him, right next to the coaster but never on it. "Any trouble from Joe's men?"

I hadn't even thought about it. "Haven't heard a peep."

"From what I can tell, they're restructuring the organization. Doesn't seem like too many men care that he's gone."

I was sure no one cared that he was gone.

"Good thing you were quick on your feet and killed all those guys. Looks like you got exactly what you wanted even though they came to kill you." He watched the TV as he drank his beer.

I'd never told him what really happened. "Actually, I didn't kill them."

"Then who did?" He turned back to me, his eyebrow raised.

"Vanessa."

"Vanessa?" he blurted, the name not sounding right as it rolled off his tongue.

"Yeah. I was on my knees and cuffed, and she came into the room with my shotgun and killed the four men. She let me have Joe."

Dumbfounded, he just stared at me. "So, let me get this straight. You're keeping that woman as a prisoner, threatening her family, and she kills the men who are about to kill you? If she'd just done nothing, you'd disappear."

"I know." I would never forget what she did for me. Not only did she save my life, but she gave me my revenge. The last thing I wanted to do was let her go, but I thought that was a fair way to repay her. Now she would never have to look over her shoulder and be afraid of me. Instead of plotting to kill her, I would always protect her. That was my way of repaying the debt.

"Am I the only one who thinks that's crazy?"

"It is crazy. I'm surprised she did it."

He drank his beer then wiped his mouth with the back of his forearm. "Looks like that woman doesn't hate you, after all…"

"She hates me now."

"Why?"

"I told her I wouldn't kill her or hurt her, out of respect for what she did to me. But I wouldn't drop the blood war…"

"Dude, she saved your life."

"And I promised I would never take hers. That's fair."

"But if she'd let you die, her family would be safe."

I drank my beer, regretting the fact that I didn't order something stronger. "Her mistake, not mine."

He chuckled then faced forward again. "You're such an asshole."

"I've never deceived her. It was her decision to save me. She didn't have to."

"Man…that woman has it bad for you."

"Bad for me?" I asked.

"She saved you because she's hung up on you. No other explanation."

The sex was hot and the chemistry was explosive, but that's all it was. She knew she wouldn't find a better man than me. If she killed me, every man who came after me wouldn't compare. She would always be unsatisfied—and she'd have to finish the job herself. "I don't know about that."

"Yes, you do."

"We haven't spoken in almost a week. Once I granted her freedom, she's wanted nothing to do with me. She's in Tuscany right now with her family."

"The family you're going to kill?"

I nodded.

"Then why are they still alive right now? You just finished one vendetta. What about the other?"

I stared at the TV without really paying attention to

it. "I told her I would reconsider my decision, and I wouldn't do anything in the meantime."

"Decision?" he asked. "To kill her family?"

I was ashamed to say the answer out loud. "Yes."

Max grinned like a boy who'd just started summer break.

"What?"

"Don't 'what' me. You fucking pussy."

"Excuse me?" I demanded.

"You're just as into her as she is into you. It's so obvious. She doesn't kill you even when she should, and now you've let her go and won't hurt her family. It's so obvious that I don't understand how it's not obvious to you."

"I like fucking her—but that's it."

"Sure. Whatever you say."

"I'm serious. Vanessa is just—"

"What's the shame in loving a woman? Come on, it's a great feeling. You find that woman you can't live without, and you enjoy her. That's not pussy shit. Pussy shit is not admitting to it."

I held his gaze, my heart thudding in my chest. "I don't love her."

"Then what is this?"

"I don't know. But I know I don't love her. I don't give a shit how beautiful she is or how much I enjoy plowing between her legs. I'll never love the daughter of the man who ruined my life. I'll never stop despising her for having everything I should have had. I respect her, but that's the extent of my feelings. So shut the fuck up and drop it."

He raised both hands in surrender. "Alright, man."

I drank my beer again, my blood boiling at the ridiculous insinuation. A man like me didn't know love. The closest I'd ever come to it was the way I felt about my mother. I was too young to remember her vividly, but I knew how it felt to be loved by someone—even if it didn't last long. I loved her in return, which was why I murdered the man who threw her in a dumpster. But I'd never come close to feeling anything in the stratosphere of romantic love. My life was about money, killing, and fucking.

That's it.

A brunette approached me at the bar, a pretty woman who would normally floor me. Long hair, a nice bust, and legs that stretched for days, she was perfect. And she had a beer in her hand, which she set right in front of me. "I was going to have the bartender send you a beer, but I wanted to bring it myself—because I definitely want to buy you a drink." Confident, she smiled at me like a woman who understood her self-worth. She wasn't shy or coy; she was just the way Vanessa was. After being with Vanessa, I'd come to realize I had a type.

I liked a strong and confident woman.

"I'm Elise." She extended her hand.

I shook it. "B."

"B?" she asked.

"Yeah. It's easier to remember that way."

She kept up her smile. "I hope you aren't involved with anyone, because I'd like to be involved with you."

Forward and aggressive, she was a little too much. "No, I'm not. You're a very beautiful woman and I appreciate the drink, but now isn't the best time for me." I turned her down right away without really thinking about what I was doing. I was horny as fuck and tired of sleeping alone, but my brain registered her as off-limits.

"That's too bad." She took the rejection with dignity. "Hopefully, the timing is better next time." She drifted away and returned to her friends in a booth.

I drank her beer even though I'd been craving something strong since my first bottle.

Max stared at me.

I felt his stare and let it continue until it couldn't be ignored. "What?"

"Nothing."

"Then why do you keep staring at me?"

"Because you've lost your mind."

I set down my beer and turned to him.

"What was wrong with her?"

"Nothing."

"Exactly," he said. "And you shot her down."

"So? I don't fuck everything that moves."

"Bullshit. Yes, you do."

"She wasn't my type. Too aggressive."

Max laughed out loud like I'd made a ridiculous joke.

"What?" I asked, dead serious.

"You only said no because of Vanessa. Let's not bullshit here. You only want her, and by definition, that means you love the woman. Because a man is only monogamous if he's in love with his lady."

"I'm not in love with her," I repeated, saying it with more conviction than before.

"You just said you haven't gotten laid all week. Vanessa is five hours away. You could be fucking that woman right now, but you're sitting here talking to me. If Vanessa really means nothing to you, then walk over there and prove me wrong."

I took a long drink of my beer before I got off the stool. "Fine, asshole." I left my money on the table to pay for my drinks before I walked away. I moved to her table and looked down at her. "Looks like I have some free time, after all."

She smiled then scooted over. "Great. Now you can buy me a drink."

THE BAR CLOSED, so we were forced to leave and move to the parking lot. Patches of snow were everywhere, and an intense chill was in the air. She was wrapped in a sweater, and I was in my leather jacket.

"So...you want to come over?" She hooked her arm through mine. "My apartment is close by."

I'd spent the evening talking to her while she ran her hand up my thigh. She got dangerously close to my dick, telling me I was going to score when the night was over. It didn't get me hard the way Vanessa did. All Vanessa had to do was tuck her hair behind her ear, and I was harder than a rock. "Sure."

She grabbed my hand and scribbled the address on my palm. "Just in case we get lost."

I walked her to her car, feeling the dread sink further and further into my chest. Deep down inside, I knew I didn't want this. I was only trying to prove something, to Max as well as myself.

The sex would be mediocre—at least for me. I wouldn't want to sleep over, so I'd have to leave in the middle of the night. And what if Vanessa called me? She probably wouldn't, but I didn't want to miss her call if she did. Even if this woman were lying beside me, I would still answer.

That was how much I wanted to talk to her.

And I would think about Vanessa the entire time I was with this woman.

Because Vanessa had covered my body in more scars than my tattoos did.

I only wanted her.

Tonight wouldn't prove anything. It was just a tedious task I was doing because I wanted to make myself feel better, to pretend that Vanessa didn't mean a damn thing to me.

She didn't mean anything to me. But that didn't mean I couldn't want just her.

"I just remembered I have to be somewhere."

"It's two in the morning…" She raised an eyebrow. "Where do you have to be?"

I had to be alone in my bed, my hand wrapped around my length to the thought of the woman I despised. "I'm married." It was a lie, but it was the easiest way to get out of this situation with the least amount of talking.

Her eyes flared in disgust. Then she slapped me across the face—hard.

It didn't feel good the way Vanessa's slaps did.

"You're a pig."

"Yeah," I said indifferently. "I know."

She got into her car and drove away.

I went home alone, getting into my big empty bed. I was eager for sex, eager for Vanessa's kisses. I wanted her nails to claw my back until she drew blood. I missed her screams as they ruptured my eardrums.

So I would just have to wait until she came back.

I knew she would call me. It was only a matter of time.

7

Vanessa

The week came to an end, and while I enjoyed spending so much time with my parents, I knew it was time for me to leave. If I stayed any longer, it would seem like I was hiding from something.

Or someone.

Mom was already hot on my trail. She knew my relationship with Bones wasn't something that could be easily swept under the rug. She didn't ask any more questions about it or make any more comments, but that wouldn't last forever.

She would bring it up again.

My father knew I had been on a date with someone that night, but he never mentioned it to me.

Thankfully.

I could talk to my mother about boys because we'd always had an open relationship. She acknowledged I was a woman when I turned eighteen. My father had never been that way. I couldn't take a boy to a school dance unless my father drove us, chaperoned the dance, and then drove us back.

I didn't mind his protectiveness because I knew he was just being a good parent. But as I got older, he remained the brooding and terrifying father figure every daughter hated. It wasn't until I moved away to school that he finally backed off.

So I really didn't want to talk about my romantic life with him.

Unless it was introducing him to the man I would marry.

Bones wasn't that man. And if he were, that would be an even bigger problem.

So my father would never ask about the man I was having dinner with. The less he knew, the better. He would live longer for it.

And if he knew what was really going on…I didn't even want to imagine.

I said goodbye to them next to my car, letting them both hold me for a long time. Mom was always sad when I left, and I could feel it in the way she squeezed me. Her hand stroked my hair, and she kissed my temple. "Come back soon."

"I will. I need to make more paintings to sell since they did so well."

Mom pulled away and smiled. "At this rate, you'll have your own gallery very soon."

I turned to my father next. "Bye, Father."

He hugged me tighter than my mother, both of his arms circling around my back as he rested his chin on my head. He held me that way for a long time, his hand rubbing my back. "*Tesoro*…call me if you need anything."

"I know, Daddy."

He kissed my forehead. "I love you more than anything."

"I know that too…"

He finally released me, an emotional look in his eyes. My father was always proud and stern around anyone who wasn't family, but when it was just us, he was vulnerable and affectionate. He wore his heart on his sleeve, and he loved me so fearlessly. It was something he only showed to other Barsettis.

"And I love you."

He opened the driver's side door. "Drive safe, alright?"

"Okay." I gave them a quick wave before I got into the car. I pulled out of the roundabout and watched them stand in the rearview mirror as I drove away. My father wrapped his arm around my mother's waist and pulled her close to him. They watched me drive away, sadness in both of their eyes.

I got onto the main road and was relieved I couldn't see them anymore. When I moved to Milan, I craved the freedom and independence. I loved living in a big city. But now that I'd been on my own for a few years, I knew the only place I wanted to be was there in

Tuscany. I wanted to live close to my parents so I could see them every day. I wanted to have that closeness I used to have growing up, when all the Barsettis were together. Carter and Conway were both in Milan, but maybe they'd reconsider moving once they settled down.

Whatever the case, I knew I wanted to be in Tuscany again—someday.

AFTER A VERY LONG RIDE, I was back in Milan.

I was tired from driving all afternoon, and now it was evening. All I wanted to do was go to bed. I'd even skip dinner because I didn't have the energy to make something or pick something up.

The streets started to look more familiar as I approached my neighborhood.

It'd been a week since I last spoke to Bones. I said goodbye to him at the car because I never wanted to see him again. I wanted our sick and twisted connection to sever in half for good. But I thought about him every day that I was gone, and I thought about him now.

A part of me wanted to drive straight to his place.

I could sleep in that comfortable bed with that strong man beside me. He would keep me warm during the night, give me the sex I'd been missing, and protect me from all the evil things in the world—except himself.

It was so tempting I almost drove past my apartment.

But I found the strength to pull into the parking lot, grab my bag and my painting, and walk inside.

My apartment was freezing, so I cranked up the heat to chase away the frost. I set my bag on the floor and leaned the wrapped painting against the wall. Even if I wanted to display it somewhere, I couldn't right now.

Not if I didn't want Bones to see it.

I normally wore a long t-shirt or a nightdress to bed, but it was way too cold for that. I pulled on thick sweatpants, a t-shirt, and a thick sweater. I hated wearing clothes to bed because it wasn't comfortable, but it was better than freezing.

And I didn't have my personal bed warmer with me.

I lay in bed in the dark and closed my eyes.

Despite the exhaustion of traveling all day, I couldn't sleep. And it had nothing to do with the freezing temperature.

I couldn't stop thinking about him.

A week of silence had distanced me from him, but that silence only made me miss him more. I wondered what he was doing while I was gone. Did he pick up a job? Or did he go out to a bar and find a woman to entertain him? Did he think about me as much as I thought about him?

He didn't call me.

Maybe he wasn't as obsessed with me as I thought he was. Maybe I was easily replaceable. Maybe my cold goodbye made him move on to someone else?

My stomach clenched in pain.

Why did I have to feel that way? Why did I have to care?

I shouldn't care.

I lay in the dark with my conflicted feelings, thinking about the man who wanted to hurt my family. If our relationship disappeared, he would have no interest in leaving my family alone. I could convince him to drop his vendetta with my silence. I wasn't a prisoner anymore, but I was still bound to him.

I tossed and turned multiple times as I tried to get comfortable, but nothing worked. This bed didn't feel right without that enormous man inside of it. I remembered the last night I stayed in this apartment and the way he camped outside in his freezing truck to keep me safe.

I'd never felt more protected as I did when he was there.

I felt invincible. More invincible than under my own father's watch.

I'd never needed a man to protect me, but now I wanted Bones to be my guard dog, to chase away evil men with just his size and ice-cold expression. Men didn't cross him, not unless they wanted to die.

He really did make my other lovers look like boys.

I hated that he was right.

I wondered if he was outside now, parked at the curb in his truck. He'd probably been watching my tracker regularly, wondering what I was doing and if it seemed like there was anything suspicious going on. When he saw my dot leave Tuscany and head north, he probably knew I was on my way back home.

So I was sure he knew I was there right now.

Maybe he was outside.

I stayed in bed and thought about it, wondering if his silver truck was parked at the curb down at the street. I couldn't close my eyes because that was all I was thinking about, wondering if that behemoth of a man was braving the freezing temperatures to keep a lookout outside my apartment.

My curiosity got the best of me, so I took my phone with me into the living room. I separated the blinds and looked outside. It took a second for my eyes to adjust to the bright light from the streetlamp. But after a moment, my eyes acclimated, and I could distinguish the street.

And his truck.

It was parked exactly where it was last time. His outline was difficult to see, but I could make out the shadow of his muscular arm and shoulder.

My heart started to race.

I could go back to bed and pretend I didn't know he was there.

But I stayed in front of the window, debating what I should do. It was freezing cold, and I didn't want to leave him outside. I didn't care that much about his discomfort; it was just an excuse. But if he was going to watch me, I'd rather it be from inside my apartment.

That was an excuse too.

All I'd been doing for the past three months with this man was make excuses.

I walked outside into the freezing cold. Despite all my layers, it wasn't enough to defend me against the frosty air that pierced right through my clothing. My arms immediately crossed over my chest, and I stood at the railing, looking down at the silver truck that contained a beast of a man.

Within seconds, his peripheral vision picked up on my movements, and he turned to gauge the situation outside my apartment. His gaze locked on mine, and he stared at me with blue eyes that reflected the frigid winter. It was a clear night and the stars were bright, but the lack of cloud cover only made it colder.

He stared at me without blinking, watching me with his usual intensity.

I'd missed it.

And I hated myself for missing it. No other man had ever looked at me that way. No other man was man enough to pull it off. Only Bones had the testosterone to make a single look so powerful. Only Bones had the strength to make a woman like me feel weak…and enjoy feeling weak.

Nothing happened as we stared at each other. He didn't get out of the truck to join me. As if he was waiting for me to go back inside, he sat absolutely still, like a mountain in a storm.

I pulled out my phone and called him.

Without taking his eyes off me, he took the call and pressed the phone to his ear. But he didn't say anything, so silent, I couldn't even hear him breathe. He had the confidence to stay quiet for long periods of time, not caring about the discomfort that stretched between him and another person.

I knew no words were forthcoming, so I spoke. "I thought you might be out here."

Nothing. Not a word.

I held his gaze, hoping he would say something. "Are you going to do this every night?"

Another pause ensued. It lasted so long I assumed he wasn't going to say anything. Eventually, he did. "You want me to leave?"

"If I said yes, would you?"

His blue eyes were pretty even this far away. "Yes. You have the power to make me do anything now. Ask me to disappear, and you'll never see me again. Ask me to stay and never leave, and you'll have me."

"Wow…that's a lot of power for one person."

Finally, the corner of his mouth rose in a smile. "I think you can handle it."

"I'm not so sure."

Another minute of silence. Another minute of direct eye contact. Another minute of me in the freezing cold.

"You should go inside."

All I had to do was walk in and forget about him, but now that I'd seen those pretty eyes that haunted my dreams, I didn't want to go inside without him. My bed suddenly felt lonelier than it ever had before. Without him beside me, it would never be comfortable again. "I will…but you should come with me."

He didn't wear a victorious expression or grin in arrogance. He hung up the phone immediately and got out of the truck, dressed in his black hoodie and black jeans. He looked up at me as he approached the stairs, his blue eyes focused on me like a target. As he came closer, his size became more enormous. His shoulders were broad, his arms were sculpted, and he was every inch of the man I remembered.

He stopped in front of me, his chin tilted down so he could look at me. He didn't touch me or kiss me, acknowledging the distance between us. A week of silence had passed, so neither one of us knew what this was anymore.

I walked inside first, and he followed.

We headed to my bedroom, and the clothes dropped to the floor behind him. His sweater made a dull thud against the floor, and his shoes were just as heavy. He stripped down to his boxers.

I turned around and looked at him, unable to take my eyes away from the enormous bulge in his boxers. Long and fat, he was as hard as ever. I was still in all my baggy clothes and without makeup, but he was harder than a steel rod.

I guessed he hadn't been with anyone else this past week. Good to know.

My eyes took in the sight of his muscled torso, of his strong pecs and his enormous shoulders. His ink contrasted powerfully against his skin, the colors so opposite that it made a beautiful sight. I'd never had an opinion about tattoos either way, and I'd never dated a guy with ink, but with Bones, I liked it. It was a big component of who he was. The ink fit him like a second skin.

I pulled my sweater over my head and then left the sweatpants behind. I kept on my long t-shirt, and it reached my thighs and covered my panties. I was excited to sleep in my own bed tonight—with my teddy bear beside me.

He got into bed first, lying back with his hand propped under his head.

I pulled back the sheets then slid between the covers. I lay beside him, not crossing the line and touching him, but close enough to take advantage of his warmth. Like laying out in the sun, just being near him was enough to get warm. He radiated heat over the sheets with the warmth that burned off his muscles, making the bedding feel like it just came out of the dryer.

I closed my eyes for a moment, feeling so comfortable that it seemed like a dream.

He turned his body toward me and lay on his side, his shoulder extending far past mine toward the ceiling. The veins along his arms were like rivers that ran all the way down to his hands. His blue eyes were on me, aggressive and soft at the same time.

I didn't touch him, but my body started to ache with desire.

My panties were getting wet. I could feel it. I wanted to moan even though his hands weren't even on me. Just being this close to him made me so aroused I could barely contain it. It must have been the last week of no action that was driving me crazy. It must have been the way his big dick looked in his boxers that made me struggle to catch my breath. I felt the heat flush into my cheeks and chest, felt my heart race in anticipation. All I had to do was lie there and go to sleep.

But damn, the last thing I wanted to do was sleep.

I opened my eyes again and looked at him, the sexiest man I'd ever laid eyes on. Dangerous and temperamental, he was the wrong guy for me. But I'd never felt more satisfied, felt more like a woman, than I did with him. And right now, my body was overriding the logic of my mind. I was getting wetter by the second, soaking my panties, and all I could think about was that cock I'd missed for the past seven days. "Bones?"

His eyes had been open the entire time, hardly blinking. He hadn't touched me, but it felt like his presence was completely wrapped around me. He was touching me with his heat, with his desire. "Yes, baby?"

"Fuck me."

He didn't smile in his typical asshole way. His eyes intensified for a brief second, and then he was up on his hands. He moved on top of me in a flash, his mouth crushing down on mine with a kiss so searing it burned my lips. "Yes, baby." He pulled my bottom lip into his mouth and dug his large hand into my hair. He possessed me immediately, like he was waiting for me to say those words the entire time. Full of restraint, he was barely holding on to his resistance. His heavy body pressed me into the mattress, and he smothered me with his size and smell. He immediately took me like I belonged to him, like I was still his even when he'd set me free.

My arms hooked over his shoulders, and I pulled him close to me, sighing in relief through my nose because it felt so right. It was so wrong, but so damn right. I breathed into his mouth and dug my nails into his fire-hot skin. My ankles locked together around his waist even though we weren't quite naked. I felt his enormous cock throb against me, felt the moisture of my panties seep into his black boxers. I wanted sex as much as this.

Whatever this was.

His kiss slowed down, less aggressive but just as passionate. He gave me his tongue and felt mine as he pulled my shirt up my belly to reveal my stomach. He pressed his defined abs against me, the hard muscles and grooves warm against my cold body. He held most of his weight on a single arm, and his thick bicep flexed with the muscles and veins.

I could feel his length right against my clit, my wetness dampening both of our clothing.

When he moaned quietly into my mouth, I knew he could feel it.

I wasn't even ashamed this time. I didn't care anymore. The past week was a pointless attempt to cut him out of my life, and since I couldn't remove him from my thoughts, the whole exercise was worthless.

"So wet, baby." He didn't stop his kiss, speaking right against my mouth.

I dragged my fingers down his back, my nails slicing into his skin. My thighs squeezed his torso, and I ground against him, excited to feel him stretch me in a way no other man ever had. The second I felt his warmth surround me, I stopped thinking about all the difficulties in my life. I didn't think about how bad this was, how terrible Bones was. I just fell into him, not thinking, only feeling. "Now, let me get you wet."

He stopped kissing me for an instant, his groan moving directly into my throat.

I pulled his boxers down so his cock and balls could be free.

He kicked them away before my thong was yanked from my body. He separated my thighs with his hips and sank me back into the mattress again. This time, he didn't kiss me. He stared into my eyes as his crown found my entrance and slid inside.

My palms pressed against his chest, and I took in a bracing breath as his cock moved deeper and deeper. Every inch was a stretch, and I felt like he was breaking me in all over again. A week without him had caused my body to tighten back up. It hurt a little more than usual, but that pain felt so good. I was out of breath and weak, so consumed with this man who was burying himself inside me.

My lips ached to say his name, to connect with him on a whole new level. I wanted him to know how good he felt, how much I let him have me. I'd never said a lover's name in bed, but I wanted to say his.

But I refused to say "Bones."

The name was evil, tainted.

"Tell me your real name." My hand slid up his corded neck and into the back of his short hair. His blond strands were soft, and they were the only soft part of his body—other than his lips.

He paused as his entire length was plunged deep inside me, my juices surrounding him and soaking him all the way through. His blue eyes burned into mine, not with hostility or anger, but with a slight hint of confusion. "Why?"

"Because I want to say your name as you fuck me." Again, the shame had been stripped away. I didn't care how wrong this was anymore. I decided to own my mistakes and be real with myself. No more lying. This was the only man I wanted in between my legs. No other man could do it the way he could. I craned my neck up and kissed him as I brought him closer to me. My ankles locked together at his back, and I rolled my hips, moving his fat dick inside me.

His breathing picked up slightly.

"Tell me." I fisted his short hair as I spoke into his mouth. His cock was so full inside me, stretching me until my entire body ached. He could hurt me so good. I loved it when he hurt me like this, made my body scream as it tried to accommodate him.

He held his massive body on his arms with ease, and he breathed into my mouth while his cock twitched inside me. His cock became gently reacquainted with my pussy, with the tightness and wetness. "Only in bed."

My heart started to race when I realized I was getting what I wanted. He'd refused to share this information with me for the past three months. It was just a name, so I didn't understand why he made a fuss about it, but to him, being referred to as Bones was important. But I would never say that name when we were like this, when we were lost in each other in bed. "Alright." My nails gently dragged down his back as I waited to hear the name he'd carried since birth, the name he'd turned his back on once he became a man.

He kissed me softly as he started to rock inside me again, to push his big cock deep before he pulled it out again. In and out he went, pushing through my wet slit with a quiet groan. "Griffin."

My ankles immediately pressed into his lower back, and my nails dug a little deeper. I stopped kissing him because all I could do was breathe. My eyes closed, and I treasured the sound of the name, turned on by the sound of his confession. He'd confided something so personal to me, and now I had a piece of him.

Just like he had a piece of me.

He positioned himself closer to me, so he could hit me deep and hard, his balls tapping against my ass with every thrust. He didn't thrust quickly, but he gave it to me at a good pace, making sure I felt him from crown to hilt before he pulled out and rammed me once more. The muscles of his torso were flexed to full capacity, the blood and muscles working together to fuck me good. His skin blushed red, and his muscles bulged like they might burst from the skin. Sweat collected on his perfect physique, the glistening forming on his neck and chest. The only thing that remained cold was the color of his eyes. They were focused on me, unblinking, like he didn't want to miss a single moment of this.

I dug my ankles into his body as I moved with him, my hands shifting to his powerful shoulders. I couldn't control my breathing because this felt too good. I'd lain in a large bed all alone for the past week, and it wasn't comfortable at all. It was cold, absent of the beast of the man who kept me warm through the night. I missed his rhythmic breathing, missed the way he was at full alert even when he was unconscious.

He widened my legs farther so he could take all of me, bury that enormous dick inside me. His chest puffed up with every deep breath he took. His eyes were on me, scorching and intense, like he was the predator and I was prey.

I was swept away in the pleasure, lost in the one man who brought me to the sky. "Griffin…" My nails cut through his skin, drawing a little blood so the salt from his sweat could sting him.

He paused for less than a second, his eyes deepening in their gaze. He let out a moan so quiet I wasn't sure if I'd really heard it. But it was just as deep as always, like a bear growling before it killed its victim. "Fuck, baby, I missed this." He pressed his forehead to mine, his hips grinding as he rubbed my clit with his pelvic bone.

My arms wrapped around his shoulders, and I felt my body convulse naturally, his movements so good. "Me too…"

He rubbed my clit a little harder before he pulled back and started to fuck me hard. He drove me into the mattress until I was practically swallowed by the pillows, sheets, and his enormous body. His thrusts were deep and hard, and his massive dick hit me in the right place every time.

God, it was so good.

He was so good.

A man had never fucked me like this before. A man

would never fuck me like this again. Even if I found the man I wanted to marry, I knew the sex wouldn't compare to what I had with this man. I would always think about him when my hand was pressed between my legs. I knew I would always want to say his name when I was with the men that came after him. He'd left his mark on me, and nothing I did could ever erase it. "Griffin…I'm gonna come." My palm cupped his cheek, my fingers feeling the chiseled bones in his jaw.

"I know, baby." He kissed me, his soft lips moving with mine. "I can feel it."

After a few pumps, he pushed me over the edge. I moaned directly into his face, my pussy tightening around him as another flood of moisture surrounded him. "Griffin…" I loved his name, loved saying it as I came all over his dick. It fit him perfectly, fit him much better than Bones ever did. My nails drew more blood, but he never voiced a single protest. In fact, it seemed like he enjoyed it.

"Fuck…" He gave his final thrusts. "I'm gonna give you so much, baby. You're going to leak all over the sheets."

"Yes…" I grabbed his hips and pulled him into me, taking as much of that cock as I could. "Give it to me, Griffin. I want it…so much." I missed the feeling of his heavy come sitting inside me, the weight so warm and good. It made me feel like a woman, to have this man's come inside me. I'd never let a man give me his seed before, and it felt so good to take his.

He gave his final thrusts then released, his entire length inside me as he exploded. I felt the heat between my legs and then the weight. It was heavier than usual, probably because there was so much of it. "Fuck…" He pressed his forehead to mine as he finished, moaning in that deep baritone.

I gripped his muscular ass and pulled him deep into me, loving the way his come sat inside me so perfectly. I loved feeling his heavy and sweaty body on top of mine, the way my nipples dragged against his chest as he moved. My nipples were chafed, but I wouldn't give up the pain, not when the pleasure was so immense.

When he finished, he looked into my eyes, his gaze dark and intense as ever.

My hands snaked up his back, feeling the line of blood I'd caused. "I'm sorry…I got carried away."

"Scratch me all you want, baby. I like it when you make me bleed." He kissed me, giving me his tongue and all of his passion, like he hadn't just come inside my wet pussy. He kept his softening dick inside me, and within a minute, it was back to full mast.

"Fuck me again, Griffin," I whispered, my voice erupting as a plea.

He kissed the corner of my mouth. "Yes, baby."

I SLEPT BETTER that night than I had all week. The sheets were warm, Bones had his arms wrapped around me with his chest pressed against my back, and the apartment felt like the safest place in the world.

I felt safer beside him than I did staying with my parents.

Even though he was a threat to everything I cared about.

I woke up rested and refreshed, and I turned over to see Bones was awake. His eyes were open, and they didn't contain the same sleepiness that I possessed, so he must have been lying there for at least an hour.

Last night came flooding back to me.

My inner thighs were still wet from his come, and the sheets underneath me were damp from where it had dripped everywhere.

He stared at me with his cold expression, his thoughts a mystery.

I stared back, seeing the lines of tattoos reaching the bottom of his neck.

His arm slid around my waist, and he pulled me closer to him, making our naked bodies come together. He hooked my leg over his hip so he could press his shaft right against my clit. He moved his hips slightly, grinding against me. "Still wet…"

"You dumped a lot in there."

He squeezed my ass cheek with his big hand. "Not enough, if you ask me."

I couldn't hold back the smile that stretched across my lips. "It's never enough with you."

"No." He kissed the corner of my mouth then my

neck. "And it's not enough with you either." He positioned me closer to him and pressed the crown of his cock inside me. He was immediately met with his come from the night before. He moaned in approval then slid farther inside until he was balls deep.

My hand pressed against his chest as I rested my face near his. I took a deep breath when I felt that impressive stretch, and I barely had the chance to breathe again before his mouth was on mine.

He kissed me as he thrust into me, his cock hitting me perfectly at this angle. His kiss never stopped as he pumped into me, and we barely moved our bodies together because we were wrapped so tightly in one another's arms.

I got off anyway, his dick so big and my clit stimulated against his body. I moaned in his mouth and then felt him dump more of his come inside me, giving me a refill to start the day. I felt its weight immediately, the warmth heating me from the inside.

He kissed me when he was finished, then gently pulled out of me, his cock acting as a plug to keep everything inside. Once it was pulled away, the come spilled from between my legs again.

He got out of bed and rose to a stand, his impressive back muscles rippling as he moved. His ink made it difficult to see where my nails had cut into him, and it was like the wounds never happened. He pulled on his boxers and walked into the bathroom.

I heard the faucet a moment later and knew exactly what he was doing.

Using my toothbrush.

I found his shirt on the ground, a dark blue V neck, and I pulled it on before I walked into the kitchen. The apartment was still a little cold despite the heater working at full capacity, so I turned it up a few degrees and made a pot of coffee. I rubbed the sleep from my eyes and stood there, thinking about what had happened.

I left town for a week to clear my head, but the second I returned, it was like nothing had changed.

Nothing had changed at all.

I left my coffee black then looked in the cabinets for something to eat.

Heavy footsteps sounded behind me, the way he announced himself before he stepped into every room. The floorboards creaked under his weight as he came up behind me. He stopped directly at my back, his breath hitting the back of my neck. He never snuck up on me, but he always made me wary whenever he was near.

"Want some coffee?" I grabbed the coffee pot and filled a mug. Steam rose from the surface as I set it on the counter beside me so he could grab it. I didn't turn around to face him directly, not wanting to meet his gaze.

"I want you." He grabbed my elbow and gently forced me to turn around. He released me when I faced him head on, my hand still gripping my mug by the handle. He grabbed his mug off the counter without looking at it and took a drink, his eyes on me the entire time.

"You drink coffee after you brush your teeth?"

"What makes you think I brushed my teeth?"

"What else were you doing in the bathroom?"

He gave me his blank stare.

"I'll pick up a new toothbrush next time I go to the store. You can keep my old one."

"We both know I'm just going to use whatever one you're using."

"Why? Why do you like my toothbrush so much?"

"Because what's yours is mine—along with everything else." He grabbed his mug again and took another drink. We stood with my back against the counter, taking up one small area inside my kitchen. His large size blocked me, kept me cornered. He conquered me in size and strength, and his massive chest was level with my gaze.

Sometimes I felt like I was in the company of a giant.

We drank our coffee as we stood there, staring at each other with mutual intensity. I'd just fucked him all night and this morning, but I wanted more. I always wanted more with this man. His sinister and criminal ways seemed unimportant in the face of my overwhelming lust. I also liked this natural connection between us, the way we could be ourselves without explanation. Bones didn't say much, but I found his silence refreshing. We could coexist peacefully in silence, our eyes doing the talking for us.

After a few minutes of comfortable silence, Bones spoke. "Sore?"

"A little."

His eyes flashed in arousal, like he was proud of the pain he'd caused. "Sorry."

"No, you aren't."

The corner of his mouth rose in a smile. "No. No, I'm not."

I brought my arms up and kept the mug level with my chest.

"If you want me to leave, you're going to have to tell me so. Otherwise, I'm not going anywhere."

I wasn't used to having a choice. Normally, I'd have to deal with Bones the way he was, stubborn and in control. But now I could ask him to stay or leave whenever I wanted. I just had a great night of sex I'd been missing, and now I could kick him out without putting up a fight. I could take advantage of it, but truth be told, I didn't want him to go anywhere.

I liked this…whatever it was.

When I didn't say anything, Bones spoke again. "How was your trip?"

"Good…it was nice to spend time with my parents."

He kept up his emotionless gaze, like that sweet confession meant nothing to him.

"I displayed my paintings at the winery, made

cookies with my mother, and spent time with my parents by the fire in the evenings. They love having me around, and they seem so heartbroken every time I leave…"

Still nothing. He didn't drop his façade of indifference, holding on to his hate despite the affectionate way I spoke of my family. "How many paintings did you sell?"

My heart picked up in speed a little bit, detecting the way he believed in me so naturally. He seemed so confident that I'd sold even one painting, and that belief meant a lot to me…more than it should. "About half…"

"I'm surprised you didn't sell them all."

I did my best to fight my expression, but it was out of my control. I felt my eyes soften before they severed the eye contact between us. "Spring is coming soon, so that should lead to more tourists…"

"Then you must have made some decent money."

"I sold each painting for about three thousand euros…"

He gave a slight smile. "Wow. That means you made at least ten thousand euros."

"Yeah…about."

"I told you that you didn't need to go to university. You're better than that. You don't need to train to be an artist. You *are* an artist." He leaned in and kissed me on the cheek, his lips soft but aggressive.

I melted at his touch, just like chocolate the second

it was popped into your warm mouth. My eyes closed, and I felt the heat circulate through me, the warmth reaching every finger and every toe. "Thanks..."

"Don't thank me," he whispered. "I'm telling you something you already know."

But I wouldn't have reached for the goal if he hadn't encouraged me to. Now I was living my dream, making art for a living. Not too many people could say that.

He set his mug down and continued to stand directly in front of me, his size backing me into the corner. The microwave was behind my head, and the stove was to my right. Everything about us was intense, from the way we spoke to each other to the way we stood near each other. Anything could happen within the span of a heartbeat.

"You brought one painting back. Why's that?"

It was the painting I'd never meant to take to begin with. My mother saw it, and now she knew I was intensely intimate with a man who didn't have a face. She'd asked me about it, and I did my best to dance around it. I didn't want to get her hopes up, that I'd found a man I wanted to introduce to the family. Bones was the last man I wanted anywhere near them. "I took it with me by mistake."

"You don't want to sell it?"

"No."

His eyes homed in on my face, as if he was searching for something.

It would only take a few seconds for him to find it.

"The painting you wouldn't let me see?"

I couldn't get the words to come out of my throat, so I just nodded.

"What are you going to do with it?"

"Not sure yet."

"Can I see it now?" he asked.

My heart started to slam in my chest, and I hoped he couldn't hear my heartbeat the way I could. "Why?"

"Why not? I'm your biggest fan, baby."

"It's just a painting…"

"If that's the case, why won't you let me see it?"

I held my mug with both hands, needing something to do with my fingertips. "It's personal…"

"My name is personal, but I shared that with you."

I dropped my gaze into my coffee, seeing the black color along with the bit of froth on top. His argument was sound, and there was nothing I could say to counter it. Perhaps I shouldn't have bothered him to share his name with me. But I wanted to know that name so badly…to say it in his ear when he pounded into me. "I'll think about it…"

"No." His quiet voice came out authoritative. "You will show it to me."

"What happened to my rights?"

"You have your rights. But you owe me. I gave you something, and now you'll give me something in return. I want to see that painting."

"It's just a painting…"

"Then it shouldn't be difficult for you to show me."

Fuck. I looked down into my coffee again. "Later… I don't want to do it right now."

Bones didn't press the argument since he finally got what he wanted. "Fine."

I set my coffee down because my hand couldn't stop shaking. I listened to it clank against the counter before I crossed my arms over my chest.

"You don't need to be afraid of me," he whispered. "I promise you I'll love it."

"That's not what I'm worried about…" I didn't want him to jump to the same conclusion my mother did. I didn't want him to see me bare my soul on that canvas. I didn't want him to see the way I viewed him, the way I stared when he wasn't looking. I didn't want him to realize how well I memorized the small details of his body, from the length of his shoulders in comparison to his waist, and the lines of ink that covered his forearms and the back of his neck. I didn't want him to see how well I captured his soul from just my memory, the way I remembered the night we met so vividly. Even if he was dense enough not to understand what my painting showed, he wouldn't be too dense to understand that I thought he was important enough to paint…that he meant something to me.

That was the last thing I wanted him to realize.

I NEVER ASKED Bones to leave, so of course, he stayed. He went to the store and picked up groceries before he returned and started to make dinner in the kitchen. I'd never asked him to do something so domesticated. He just left, didn't tell me where he was going, and when he came back, dinner was cooking on the stove.

He showered, but he remained in his boxers all day, choosing to dress minimally despite the cold temperature of my apartment. The frost never bothered him, regardless of how cold it was. His internal mechanism kept him warm no matter what the conditions were.

I sat at the window and painted on my canvas, taking advantage of the last bits of sunlight before it disappeared altogether. I wore his t-shirt along with a sweater and my jeans, trying to stay warm even though the heater was working at full capacity.

I listened to the sound of the sizzling pan and smelled the meat as it cooked on the stove. Bones hadn't said a word to me in several hours.

We coexisted—peacefully.

He walked into the living room and suddenly pulled out some firewood from the grocery bags. He set everything in the fireplace, lit it with a match, and then turned it into a billowing fire within minutes. He fanned it for a bit before the flames were steady. Then he dusted his hands and walked back into the kitchen.

I was so glad he couldn't see my face. My hand shook as I held the paintbrush, the terror gripping my heart. Only people innately comfortable with each other could enjoy the silence and not feel pressured to fill it with meaningless words. Our interaction reminded me of my parents, who didn't say a lot to each other when they were together throughout the day. I'd seen them eat dinner together on the terrace, not exchanging a single word. It wasn't because they didn't enjoy each other's company—it was because they enjoyed it so much.

Bones and I reminded me of them, of a man and a woman living their lives together. He shopped for groceries, built me a fire when I was cold, and he made dinner in the kitchen since cooking wasn't my forte.

What the hell was this?

I dropped my brush into the water glass and sat there, looking at my painting without really caring about it. I felt the flames keeping me warm on my left and listened to Bones move around in the kitchen. He had a gorgeous apartment ten minutes away that was ten times bigger than this, and he had a beautiful mansion in the snow, but he chose to be here with me— even when we weren't screwing.

This was so fucked up.

Bones brought everything to the coffee table, the only surface I had for eating. My place was too small for a kitchen table, not if I wanted to have two couches. I never sat at the dinner table when I ate alone anyway, so it seemed like a waste.

He must have picked up on my mood because he

asked, "What is it, baby?"

Baby. He called me that every chance he got, and now I didn't remember how my real name sounded on this tongue. "Nothing…" I turned away from my easel and rose from the stool.

He gave me a stern look, telling me he didn't believe that answer at all.

"This looks good…" I sat on the floor in front of my plate, keeping my eyes away from his so he couldn't look into my soul.

Thankfully, he dropped it and walked back into the kitchen. He returned with everything else then sat across from me.

We ate in silence—just like my parents.

Why was this happening? How did this happen? How the hell did we get here?

He drank scotch with his dinner, while I had a glass of wine with mine. He used both utensils to cut into his food, and he ate his meal like a refined man with manners. It was in direct contrast to how barbaric he normally was. But when it came to food, he was the most civilized.

"This is really good." I was surprised he cooked so well. It was nothing compared to the meals Lars made for me, but it was far superior to anything I could make. "Thanks for making dinner." I tried to fill the silence with conversation, tried to break the comfortable atmosphere. I didn't want it to feel so right, to feel so easy.

He turned his blue gaze on me and watched me, subtly hostile. He chewed slowly, his expansive shoulders broad and powerful. He sat perfectly upright, so my eyes still had to shift up in order to look at him. He didn't say anything, forcing the silence to continue.

Goddammit. I grabbed my wine and took a deep drink.

"What is it?" he repeated.

"What?" I asked, playing dumb.

"You're too smart to act stupid. Don't pull that shit with me." He stared me down before he took another bite of his food.

I didn't want to tell him the truth, not before I showed him that painting. So I shared something else with him. "My mom told me the owner of that restaurant we went to is good friends with my father…and he told my parents that he saw me on a date with a really handsome man."

He didn't give me an arrogant smile at my comment. He stayed hostile, his light-colored eyes aggressive.

"She asked me who the man was…I didn't tell her."

"And that was the end of it?"

"She said a few other things, asked me to talk about it. I've always been pretty open with her about my personal life. I told her about my first crush, my first kiss…stuff like that. My father has always been overbearing, but my mother has never been that way."

"But you couldn't talk about me to her."

"I wouldn't even know what to say…and I hate lying to her."

"Then don't lie," he said simply.

"You know I can't do that…"

He took a long drink of his scotch, keeping his eyes on me.

"I hate being so secretive, but I have no choice. When she reminded me that she and my father would like to meet someone I'm seeing, I told her that wasn't necessary. My father implied he would only want to meet the man I'll probably marry…and I told her you weren't that man. Hopefully, that put it to rest." I drank my wine again, hoping my story was enough to persuade him that he meant nothing to me. I had to poison the well while I had a chance. When he saw that painting, I didn't know what would happen.

His expression didn't change at all. That information didn't mean anything to him. He drank his scotch again. "You don't have to lie to her if you don't want to. You could always ask me to leave and never come back. Then there would be nothing to lie about." He must have known I wouldn't do that. If that were a possibility, he wouldn't still be in my apartment, cooking dinner and pretending everything was perfectly normal.

I drank my wine again, a pathetic attempt to cover my silence.

"It's okay, baby. I'm just as addicted to you as you are to me."

I didn't want to go out and meet someone new. I

didn't want to picture myself with another man. All I wanted was this…but he was evil. He was a threat to my family and everything that I cared about. How could I possibly want his company, in and out of bed? "What did you do while I was away?" I wanted to talk about anything but the obviously fucked-up situation between us.

"I had a hit in Budapest. Then I went out with Max a few times." He cut into his food again.

"How'd it go? The hit?"

"I was in and out in thirty minutes. Did my job, then got paid."

I was still repulsed by what he did for a living. I wanted to say it out loud, but I didn't want him to throw out accusations that my family wasn't any better. "Did you get hurt?"

The corner of his mouth rose in a smile. "I like it when my baby worries."

I looked down at my food and took a bite. "Did you?"

"Don't worry, not a scratch."

"And where did you go with Max?"

"A few bars." He dropped his smile and turned serious. "Spent most of my time wondering when you would be back."

"Why didn't you call?"

"I was under the impression you didn't want me to."

I didn't…but I did. I'd wanted to call him a few times, but I refused to stoop to that level. But the second

I was home, I did anyway. "Did you hook up with anyone?" I hated myself for asking that question. I hated myself for caring. But I did care. It tore me up inside to think about him being with another woman. A man like him could have any woman he wanted. He didn't even have to open his mouth and speak, and they'd hop into bed with him.

Instead of smiling in arrogance, he just a gave a subtle shake of his head. "No."

I tried to mask the deep breath I pushed out of my lungs, but I knew nothing escaped his notice. He already knew I was jealous. Insanely jealous. Like, red in the face kinda jealous.

"I said no. But good to know you still want my answer to be no."

"I didn't say anything."

"But you were getting pissed. It's been three months, baby. I know you. I know you better than you want me to know you."

I wanted to pick up my plate and throw it at his head. I hated this. I hated everything about it. And I hated the fact that he was right.

We finished our dinner in silence, back to our comfortable coexistence. When his plate was empty and most of my food was gone, he cleared the dishes and took them to the sink.

"I'll wash them since you cooked."

He didn't give a protest and walked into the living room to turn on the TV.

I scrubbed everything and put it in the dishwasher, but I despised myself for doing it. Now we had a routine—like a fucking married couple.

I grabbed one plate and slammed it into the sink, making it shatter with a bang.

Bones didn't come back into the room.

I stared at the broken plate and listened to the water run. Bones had given me my freedom, but it didn't make any difference. I'd never been his prisoner. I'd always been a prisoner to myself. I could ask him to leave, but I didn't want to.

I wanted him to stay.

Bones came to my side then picked up the pieces of plate without asking what happened.

"I can take care of it."

"I don't want you to cut your hands. You need them to paint." He picked up everything, nicking himself without expressing a hint of pain. He tossed everything in the garbage then went back into the living room so he could watch TV.

I finished the dishes then returned to the living room. He was lying on the couch, all muscle and power. His ink contrasted against his beautiful skin, and the glow from the fire made the tattoos stand out even more.

My knee hit the couch, and I prepared to lie on top of him, my favorite place to rest while watching TV in the evenings.

But he steadied me with his hand and sat up. "We

had a deal." He sat back against the couch and stared at me with his innate power, reminding me of the agreement we'd made earlier that morning.

Was I stupid to hope he would forget?

He kept staring at me, waiting for me to do what he asked.

I sighed through my nose, irritated that so much was going wrong. I went to my parents' house to clear my head, but now my mind was even more foggy.

"Now."

I wanted to slap him across the face for making the command, but since he would only enjoy it, I walked into the bedroom and picked up the painting. I didn't unwrap it for him, wanting to make it as difficult as possible for him to see what I'd created.

I set it down next to the couch then turned for the bedroom.

"Where are you going?"

I halted before I reached the hallway, keeping my back to him. "You said you wanted to see the painting. There it is."

"Get your ass back here."

I should just keep walking, but I didn't.

"Don't make me ask you again."

"What happened to my free will?"

"Doesn't apply here. Whatever fear you have about this painting needs to be conquered. You should never feel ashamed of anything you make. Without even looking at it, I know it'll be stunning."

I closed my eyes. "You don't understand…"

"I understand better than you think. Now, get over here."

I finally turned around and walked back to the couch.

He nodded to the seat beside him.

I obeyed him, and I felt so pathetic doing it. I sat on the couch beside him, feeling the heat emitting from his bare torso. He couldn't read my mind, but looking at that painting was like glimpsing into my deepest thoughts. I should have just sold it or burned it. Or better yet, I shouldn't have painted it in the first place.

Bones looked at me for a moment longer before he grabbed the large painting and placed it across his lap. He carefully tore the brown paper away from the frame and stripped away every piece until all the coverings were removed. He hadn't looked at the painting yet because he was too busy concentrating on preserving the frame.

He tilted it up, held it with both hands, and finally looked at it.

I could have sworn that my heart stopped beating.

He stared at the image in front of him, his eyes wide open and not blinking. The fire crackled in the background, the low-burning flames casting a glow that constantly changed as the fire rose and fell. The TV was off now, so all I could hear was our breathing and the fireplace.

His eyes hadn't left the painting, taking it in just as

he did with my other pieces. He wasn't an art aficionado, but he appreciated the art in front of him. His eyes naturally followed the lines I created, and he stared at the representation of himself as he stared across the lake.

There was no mistaking it was him.

He didn't seem surprised to see himself. He didn't seem surprised by the image I decided to paint. His face was impossible to read, focused like I wasn't even there at all. His eyes started to shift around, to stare at the details of the trees and the texture of the snow. Then his eyes moved to the water in the distance, the small dock that extended twenty feet into the lake. He'd just dropped a body there, but there wasn't a hint of that in the painting. The van wasn't in sight, and I wasn't there either.

It was just him.

It cast him in a light he didn't show often, a likeness of himself as a man instead of a killer. He appreciated the view around him like any man would, and his broad shoulders seemed to be weighed down by a pain only he could see.

I saw him in a way no one else did. He picked up women all the time, but they only saw his handsome face, impressive physique, and his sexy ink. They didn't know about his past, his occupation.

I knew about all those things, but it didn't stop me from looking at him like that.

Like he was just a man.

I saw all of him, from the boy who lost his mother, to the man who wanted to avenge his legacy. I saw in him all the good and all the bad. I accepted him for who he was, even accepted his flaws.

Accepted his blood war.

Could he see all of that as he looked at the picture? Could he see my affection, my need for him? Could he see everything I'd been trying to hide?

Thirty minutes passed, and he still seemed enamored of the picture, looking at every detail like he might have missed something. He didn't say a single word to show his opinion, and his expression didn't give anything away either.

When he finished, he put it on the floor and leaned it against the coffee table.

My heart was beating so fast I could feel the blood pound in my ears. I felt weak and terrified, unsure what Bones would think about my creation. It obviously meant something to him because he wouldn't have stared at it for so long.

He shifted forward with his elbows on his knees, his eyes looking at nothing in particular. His jaw was clenched, not in anger, but with tension. His hands came together, and he rubbed them slightly.

I waited for him to say something, but it didn't seem like anything was going to be said. Our silence used to make me feel comfortable, but now it was making me anxious. I didn't know if he was thinking about walking out the door or staying beside me. I didn't know where we stood anymore. I could usually feel whatever he was feeling—but this time, I didn't have a clue.

Finally, his baritone broke the silence. "That's how you see me?" He finally turned my way, his beautiful blue eyes looking into mine. His look wasn't cold but seared me like a flame. There wasn't a trace of hostility or rage.

He'd asked a question, but I wasn't sure if it was a genuine one. "It's just a painting…"

"It's not just a painting, baby," he whispered. "That must have taken you a long time to make. When I looked at it, I could feel the cold… I can feel my breath escape as vapor. I could feel the way that bullet pierced my shoulder." He rubbed the area, like the bullet was still lodged deep inside his flesh. "I could feel the way my lips burned when I kissed you for the first time. I could feel the deep loneliness inside my chest, that solitude I feel anytime I'm up in Lake Garda. I could feel the way you fought me, the way you impressed me when you crawled across the ground because that taser had no effect on you. I relived that entire night, but more vividly than when I actually lived it."

My eyes moved down, touched by everything he just said.

"Look at me."

I didn't think twice before I obeyed, my eyes shifting back up to look at him.

"That's how talented you are," he whispered. "That's how powerful you are."

"Powerful?" I whispered.

"You made me feel something... You always make me feel something. You manipulate my emotions without even realizing it. I've seen all of your artwork, and I know the only people you ever depict are your family."

Shit.

"But you painted me..."

No. No. No.

I looked away again, unable to see the knowledge in his eyes.

"Baby."

This time, I wouldn't look at him again.

"Don't be afraid of me."

"It's not you that I'm afraid of..."

"Don't be afraid of us."

I closed my eyes, wishing all of this would stop. I felt so much guilt, so much rage. I didn't want to be there in that moment. I didn't want to be stuck in this sick and twisted situation. If only he said or did something that could sever our ties altogether, everything would be so much easier.

"I asked you to make that painting for me so I would always have a piece of you. I want to put it in my office in Lake Garda. That way I can remember what we had. I can stare at it while I drink my scotch and smoke my cigars. I want to remember how all of this felt...and never forget. Because you aren't like any other woman I've ever been with, Vanessa. And I know I'm not like any other man you've been with. When all of this is over…we'll both never forget what we had."

I opened my eyes again, relieved that he didn't see more into the painting. I didn't want him to think I wanted forever, that I wanted this perverse arrangement to continue indefinitely. We were both addicted to each other, addicted to the good sex and the scorching chemistry. One day, we would walk away from each other. Bones might be my enemy forever, and I would have to face him across a battlefield. Or he would let this blood war go, and he would disappear from my life.

Either way, the outcome was the same.

There was no future for us.

He understood that. I understood that.

These paintings were just snapshots of moments in time. They showed the way we viewed each other, the way we wanted to remember one another.

"You really know me," he whispered. "Better than anyone…"

"I do?"

He nodded. "And I think I know you better than anyone too."

I wanted to tell him that wasn't true, that it would never be true. My biggest enemy was my closest confidant. He was the man I shared all things with, including my body. But an argument was futile, so there was no point in denying it.

I had to accept the painful truth—and try to swallow it.

8

Bones

I had a lot of different hobbies.

I liked to kill.

Drink.

Fuck.

And watch sports.

That was pretty much everything.

But now I had a new hobby, a hobby I acquired three months ago.

Vanessa Barsetti.

I sucked her clit into my mouth and gave it a gentle bite before I swirled my tongue around her nub, tasting her beautiful pussy. My tongue delved into her slit, reaching the moisture that had already pooled for me a long time ago. A man usually went down on a woman to make her wet, but with my baby, I didn't need to do that.

She was already soaked.

I did it because I enjoyed it, enjoyed listening to her breathe into the darkness of her bedroom. Her small hands would clamp on to my wrists and hold on as I pressed my nose into her slit and smelled her.

She arched her back and bucked her hips automatically.

I sucked her clit again before I crawled up her body and brought her nipple into my mouth. I sucked hard, sucked until it was raw. I moved to the other tit and did the same. I worshiped every part of her body, dragging my tongue into the valley between her tits before I breathed into the hollow of her throat. I'd taken her so many times, but every time I explored her body, it felt like a new experience.

I tortured her on purpose, not kissing her or fucking her so she would writhe underneath me. But it was torturing me too, because I wanted to take her as much as he wanted to have me.

It was horrific to us both.

I finally made my way up her body until my lips hung just inches away. My knees separated her thighs, and I pressed my shaft against her throbbing clit. I looked into her eyes, but all I could see was that painting.

That painting she made of me.

She gripped my shoulders and breathed in my face, anxious and desperate. "Griffin…please."

A beautiful woman like her shouldn't have to beg. "Yes, baby." I widened her thighs farther and pressed my crown through her slit, feeling the squeeze as I pushed through. She was wet from my saliva as well as her own arousal. It made my entry smooth and less painful for her. But my thick cock could still do some damage, regardless of how wet she was. I sank into her warm flesh until I was buried deep inside, nearly touching her cervix. "I love this pussy…"

Her fingers moved through my hair, and she breathed with me, her chest rising and falling in sync with mine. "She loves you too." She kissed the corner of my mouth before she went for the deeper embrace, moving her lips against mine with passion.

I started to thrust and listen to the sound our bodies made together. Her pussy was so wet that I could feel us slide past each other. Her cream built up along my base, pushing down with every stroke until it built up at my hilt and just behind the groove at the head of my dick.

I loved her cream.

She kissed me as I moved with her, her thighs hugging my waist.

The second she'd returned from Tuscany, I'd been just like this with her. I'd taken her over and over again, feeling satisfied when we were finished but even more desperate for her after an hour had passed. She was a quick fix, but I always came back wanting another.

If I'd slept with that other woman, whatever her name was, it wouldn't have been like this.

Nothing like this.

She would have enjoyed it the way Vanessa did, but

I wouldn't be so hard. I wouldn't be aroused. I wouldn't feel like such a man because any woman besides Vanessa just wasn't woman enough for me.

Only Vanessa was.

She hated me for the demon that I was, for the promise I made to annihilate her family. But her hatred only went skin-deep, and underneath that were emotions more complex than either of us could understand.

The best explanation was her painting.

The way she saw me.

I wasn't a murderous criminal that wanted to hurt her family. I was a man alone in the world, isolated from love, friendship, and community. I didn't have a single relative, and all I had were the boys I did business with. I didn't have a woman who loved me or children to remember me when I was gone.

I was alone.

So fucking alone.

She saw that. She saw the conflict inside me. She knew I needed revenge to find peace, but every completed vendetta would bring me back to the same place.

Solitude.

But I loved that she understood me—and accepted me.

So why would I want to have some woman I found in a bar? Whether she was more beautiful or not, she wasn't Vanessa.

No woman could even come close.

I drove her into a climax almost instantly since I'd spent so much time torturing her. She screamed in my face and clawed at me, drawing blood just like last time. Her thighs squeezed me hard, and she bucked against me, enjoying my fat cock and all the pleasure it was giving her.

I watched the production she put on, entranced by the expression she made when she came around my dick. Her eyes squinted hard, and her jaw tensed for second before her mouth opened with a scream. The flood of color entered her cheeks, and when her eyes opened again, they were brighter than before. She watched my expression, and like my stare turned her on even more, she finished the orgasm with another round of convulsions.

Beautiful.

Fucking beautiful.

SHE WAS asleep when I crept out of bed and walked into the living room. I shut the door behind me, poured a glass of scotch, and got the fire going again. When I glanced at the clock on her wall, it said it was three in the morning.

Normally, I could sleep like a rock with Vanessa. Her soft skin, feminine smell, and the way her hair touched my skin when she turned over were all comforting to me. Her hands were always on me, feeling me in the dark to make sure I was still there. Even when she was dead asleep, my presence was important to her. I kept her warm throughout the night so she didn't have to wear those baggy clothes that made her shapeless, and I protected her from all the things that terrified her.

I was her rock.

But tonight, sleep eluded me. I kept thinking about that painting she'd made. It haunted me so much that I couldn't sleep. I kept thinking about the colors, how the scenery looked exactly as it had on that night. She didn't have a picture to work off like she usually did—it was all from memory.

How the fuck did she do that?

I sat on the couch and lifted the painting onto my lap. It wasn't a small canvas, but a medium size, something that could be placed on a living room wall. I leaned back and stared at it, studying the black hoodie I wore and the part of the skull tattoo that rose up the back of my neck.

She knew my tattoos as well as I did.

The jeans were the same ones I'd been wearing that night, even the shoes. There was never a time when I actually stopped to look at the water, but I'd done it before. I'd stood there and looked across the frozen lake countless times, thinking about all the dead bodies I'd sunk to the bottom.

The snow was the perfect texture, a mixture of

powder and slush. The trees were the exact type that stood there, tall with a path that led directly to the water. The leaves were gone because winter had been too unforgiving that year. She captured a vista I'd been looking at for a decade—but she only saw it one time.

My image was the most striking. It didn't show my face, but it showed my outline perfectly. Even the way I stood was correct, the way I slid my hands into my front pockets when I was the least hostile.

This woman knew me.

Now that I could see how she stared at me, I felt like I saw something else, something more meaningful. She'd spared my life once before, saved my life another, and even though I said I continued to want to kill her family…she was still there.

And I was still there.

I'd never been with one woman for so long. This was a marathon compared to all the others, but I wasn't eager to finish the race. I loved it when she got jealous. I loved it when she asked me to be all hers.

I loved it when she felt safe when I was there.

I loved it when she got jealous just from wondering what I did while she was gone.

I loved how she hated it when I left.

I loved how she tried so hard to cut me out of her life but couldn't do it.

I loved it all.

What did that say about me?

I WENT to my place down the road. It'd been cleaned up after Joe tried to kill me, and even though I thought about that night every time I stepped out of the elevator, it didn't bother me enough to seriously consider moving.

I refused to let an asshole fuck with me—especially after he was dead.

I made myself a cup of coffee and then went into my office. I had paperwork to go over, shit that came with the business when we were researching potential hits.

An hour later, Vanessa called me.

I leaned back in my chair and answered. "Hey, baby."

"Where are you?" She blurted out the question like she had every right to ask it.

I couldn't keep the grin off my face. "Home."

"I didn't know you were leaving…"

I'd left in the morning long before she woke up. I didn't say goodbye or leave a note. Staring at the painting all night excited me and terrified me. I enjoyed fucking her so much that I didn't really think about what we were doing.

I should have killed her a long time ago—but I never did.

She should have killed me—had several chances.

She ruined my plans, and I ruined hers.

When I took a step back and thought about all of it, I realized we were both in deep shit.

"I have stuff to take care of."

"Oh…"

I'd never just left like that. Most of the time, I didn't leave unless I took her with me. But I didn't want to be there any longer, not when I was confused like this.

That painting was crystal clear—but fucking confusing.

The silence lingered on the phone between us, growing louder and louder.

"I feel like there's something wrong." She conveyed her honest truth to me, showing her vulnerability more and more. "Is there…?"

"No, baby. I just…need some space right now." She'd asked for space after I kept my vendetta against her family even though she'd saved my life. I wasn't sure what she'd thought about during that week we were apart, but it seemed like nothing had changed. Now it was my turn to consider this strange relationship.

"It's because of the painting, isn't it?" She sighed into the phone, the pain heavy in her voice.

I wanted to lie and say that wasn't true, but I told her I would always be honest with her. "Baby, you asked me to keep a promise. Do you remember what it was?"

She was quiet for a long time, not because she couldn't remember, but because she didn't want to say it out loud. "I asked you never to leave me…"

"And I promised I wouldn't. I'm not going anywhere. I just need some time."

More silence.

I stayed on the line, unsure what else could be said at this point.

"I thought you said you weren't the kind of man who kept promises?"

No, I wasn't. All I cared about was money and sex, not my reputation. "I'm not. But I always keep my promises to you."

MAX STEPPED inside my office and tossed the large yellow folder at me. "It's all there."

I ripped open the top and slid the papers onto the table. I looked at the photos and itinerary, along with the information about security and the number of men at each place and the kind of weapons they were packing.

Max helped himself to the scotch as he sat across from me. "Are you sure you want to do this? It seemed like you had a good thing going with Vanessa."

I picked up the photo of Conway Barsetti and examined it, seeing him holding hands with his fiancée outside the old theater in the center of Milan. He was dressed in a black suit that fit his sculpted shoulders and thick arms. He didn't smile, and I'd never seen him smile in public or real life. His fiancée, on the other hand, couldn't look happier. Her baby bump stuck out just a little bit.

"He's going to be at a show next Saturday. Debuting a new line of lingerie. It's going to be here in Milan. I managed to grab all the security information from my buddy. I know who's on his crew and what they'll be carrying."

"Good." Conway Barsetti took his team everywhere he went, not just because of the paparazzi, but because he knew he had enemies everywhere. People were naturally envious of billionaires.

Max continued to stare at me as he drank his scotch. He wiped his mouth with the back of his forearm. "You're actually going to do this?"

My perfect shot was next Saturday. Conway would exit out of the back of the building and into his SUV. Little would he know, I would be waiting for him. I'd take him and his fiancée prisoner, and I would do the very thing I couldn't do to Vanessa—slit their throats. It would start the blood war—and the Barsettis would come after me.

But they would be so delirious with rage they wouldn't be able to think clearly.

They'd expose themselves—and I would murder each one.

Except Vanessa.

"I'm thinking about it," I answered.

"I don't know a lot about the Barsettis, but the two

brothers have dark pasts. They've annihilated every enemy they've ever had."

"I'm aware," I said coldly.

"And Vanessa saved your life."

"Her mistake."

Max narrowed his eyes on my face. "I admire your determination and your refusal to let pussy get in the way of your vendetta, but this isn't going to be a simple kill like it was with Joe. This is much more complicated because there are so many Barsettis. They're loyal to each other. And the second you turn on them, Vanessa will turn on you. She won't hesitate to pull the trigger this time."

"I'd judge her if she didn't."

His eyes fell in disappointment. "I'm not helping you with this. It's just going to get me killed."

"That's fine. I never asked for your help."

He downed the rest of his scotch and left the glass on my desk. "Good luck, Bones." He left my office and helped himself to the elevator. Once the sound of the machinery died away and everything turned quiet, I knew I was alone.

I spread out the different pictures of the Barsetti family, looking at their files with a keen eye. The men were all similar, sharing the Barsetti bloodline with dark hair, green eyes, and Tuscan skin. The wives were much fairer, softer. When I looked at Crow and Pearl Barsetti, I saw a photographic combination of Vanessa's features. She possessed her mother's softness and her father's might. She took her mother's angled face and inherited her father's eyes. These two people made the most beautiful woman in the world.

I looked at the last picture, the one of Vanessa. It was a picture of her at university, walking across campus with her bag over her shoulder. She stared directly ahead of her, not looking down at her feet like most other students did. She carried herself like nobility, as if she understood her self-worth. She commanded respected naturally, not just because of her beauty, but because of her grace.

I put the picture in a different pile because she was off-limits.

I spared her life.

Even if she tried to kill me, I wouldn't hurt her.

If the Barsettis really wanted to put me down for good, Vanessa was their best weapon. She wore an invisible bulletproof vest. She had a wall of protection around her no one could see. She had supernatural powers—because I was defenseless against her.

I wanted to continue this vendetta and put my enemies in the ground. I wanted to avenge the legacy I'd lost. I wanted repayment for the inheritance that was given to someone else. I wanted payback for the years of hell my mother and I suffered.

But if I went through with it, it would devastate the one woman I cared about.

The one woman who cared about me.

My thoughts circled in my mind over and over

again, making me think the same things I'd already thought a million times before. That painting was burned in my memory now because I'd stared at it for so long.

That painting changed everything.

But I didn't want anything to change.

I didn't want this woman to consume me like this, to claw her way into my chest and stay there. She had an invisible hold over me, but as time passed, that power became more visible. My cock stayed in my pants when she wasn't around, not out of obligation but desire. I put the war on hold because I wanted to give her peace. I was sleeping in the same woman's bed every night, when I never slept with anyone.

She had me wrapped around her finger.

But I had her wrapped around mine too.

I piled everything together and placed it on the side of my desk, unsure what I should do with it. Before I made my official move, there was something I needed to do first.

I needed to go to Lake Garda.

And stand in the very place where she painted me.

MY SHOES CRUNCHED against the snow as I walked down the bank toward the water. It was freezing the same way it was that night. The sun was almost gone, so the sky was a mixture of light colors, pink, blue, and a dash of orange. Within minutes, all traces of sunlight would be gone.

I stopped in the exact place where I stood in the painting and stared at the water. I watched the dock rise and fall slightly with the moving lake, and I stared at the trees around me. Like I was standing in the picture, I saw everything exactly as she depicted, from the number of trees in the clearing to the number of leaves that remained on each branch.

I felt like I was standing inside her mind.

Every breath I took was accompanied by the painful bite of the frozen temperatures. It burned my lungs on the way in, and when I breathed out again, my breath escaped as vapor. I watched it rise up in front of my face before it disappeared into the frozen air.

My hands moved into my pockets, and I cherished the cold, cherished the way it penetrated my clothes and to my warm muscles. Slowly, the sun disappeared from the horizon, and the pretty colors faded.

Now the light was limited.

It started to turn into that night, that night when I met Vanessa in an alleyway. I was going to kill her, but then I caught a glimpse of her face and recognized her. I should have killed her anyway, but my enemy deserved a better death than that.

I wanted her to know who I was first.

But now, the last thing I wanted to do was kill her.

I wanted to be in bed with her, in that small apartment with no food in the kitchen. Her bed was small and uncomfortable, and she kept the place a few degrees too warm for me. But I wasn't there for the comfort. I was there for the woman.

Now I was confused about what I wanted.

About what this woman meant to me.

I couldn't kill her, not just because she'd saved my life, but because I didn't want to. I never wanted to hurt her. She asked me not to tie her up, and I actually listened to her. I got scared when I saw her walking down the sidewalk of a busy road, so I went to check on her and was grateful I had. I chased those assholes away.

All I wanted to do was protect her.

But how could I protect her and kill her family at the same time?

I had to choose.

Vanessa or my vendetta.

I couldn't have both.

9

Vanessa

When Bones left without saying goodbye, it hurt.

He'd never done that before.

Most of the time, I couldn't get rid of him. He made my sheets smell like him, left his coffee mug in the sink, and used my toothbrush like it was his. He invaded my space like a bad roommate and left his clothes on my bedroom floor. He made his mark everywhere, from my things to my actual skin.

But when he left, I felt empty.

I didn't like it when he wasn't there.

When I went to bed for the next two nights, I tried not to be scared of whatever lingered outside my apartment. But my longing got the best of me, and I peeked out the window in the hopes I would see his truck at the curb.

But it wasn't.

I reminded myself that he wouldn't leave me if he thought I was actually in danger.

He would always protect me.

But I still hated the fact that he was gone, hated sleeping in a million layers while the bed still remained cold. I missed his smell. I missed his powerful arms wrapped around me. I missed the sex before we went to sleep.

God, this was bad.

I'd left Milan to clear my head, and once I returned, I was all over him again. Now that he was gone, I couldn't stop thinking about him. As if I was losing my mind until I could get my next fix, I was anxious and desperate.

I was so damn attached to him.

How could I be attached to a man who wanted to hurt my family?

I hated myself. I hated myself so much. I judged myself for getting into this situation. I judged myself for not letting him die like I should have. I judged myself for feeling so many emotions for this man.

What was wrong with me?

The painting pushed him away. He saw the emotion I infused into the paintbrush. He took it as a confession, that I was pinned under his thumb so well that he could do anything he wanted to me. I was attached to him, desperate for him. He kept me as a prisoner at the time, but that painting showed I never felt like a prisoner.

I wanted him so bad.

He didn't know what to do with that information, so he left.

I couldn't blame him.

I should I could leave too.

Maybe I would get lucky, and he would decide to break things off between us. Maybe he would find a different woman, and the pain of his betrayal would be enough to make me return to my family and tell them we needed to kill Bones.

But he promised he would never leave me, that he would always come back to me. I was consoled by those words when I wished I weren't, but I hung on to that confession like a lifeline. It reassured me that we still belonged to one another, that we couldn't live without each other.

A part of me wished he would break that promise.

A bigger part of me never wanted him to.

Three days came and went, and I didn't hear from him. I spent my time working on my paintings and cleaning the apartment. The painting I made of him was hung on my bedroom wall, so I could see it at night when I went to sleep. It made me feel safe, even though Bones couldn't jump out of the painting and protect me.

Sleeping without him got easier, but it was never the same as it was when I had him by my side. I missed the way his weight sank into the mattress and forced me to roll toward him. I missed the way he put his stuff on his nightstand, making himself at home. But I pushed through it, telling myself I was being pathetic for letting his absence bother me this much

I didn't want to be that kind of woman.

I'd always been strong, with or without a man.

But when it came to this one man…everything was different.

He made me so damn weak.

It was almost nine in the evening when I got a text message from him. *I'm coming inside in five minutes.* He never warned me when he was coming over, but I knew this was because I was a little timid at night. Just the slightest sound kept me up for an extra hour because I couldn't figure out what caused it.

I didn't text back, and I stayed on the couch, knowing I would hear his footsteps before he reached the door. I turned off the TV and let the fire crackle in the fireplace. My eyes moved to the window, waiting for his shadow to appear.

A few minutes later, I saw his silhouette through the curtains and heard his heavy footsteps against the concrete. He approached the door, slipped a key into the lock, got it open, and then stepped inside.

He locked the door behind him, dressed in a gray hoodie with black jeans. His black ink peeked out from underneath his sleeves. He stopped in the living room and stared at me, his bright eyes full of intensity. He stared at me just the way he always did, like nothing had changed between us despite his absence.

After a few seconds of holding his gaze, I rose to my

feet and walked toward him. I was in black leggings and a baggy long-sleeved t-shirt, ready to go to bed when I couldn't keep my eyes open anymore. I didn't have any makeup on, and the curls in my hair had fallen out since this morning.

He glanced at my lips but didn't kiss me.

I didn't touch him either, unsure what he was thinking or feeling.

Finally, his hand slid around my waist while his other palm cupped my cheek. His fingers gently pushed my hair back, and his callused thumb rubbed against my soft skin. His face moved closer to me, his eyes focusing on mine.

The second he touched me, I turned soft. I closed my eyes and felt the warmth of his palm. I turned my cheek into it, loving the way his hand felt against my skin. I loved the way his fingertips gripped the back of my shirt as he held me. I closed my eyes and treasured all of it, missing this touch deeply.

He pressed his face to mine and kissed the corner of my mouth. His lips were soft and gentle, and when they took mine, they were full of possession and longing. He gently pulled my bottom lip into his mouth, released it, and then kissed me again. He gave me this tongue, but it was in an affectionate way instead of lustful. He kissed me harder then pulled away unexpectedly to place his mouth against my ear. "I missed you…"

"I missed you." My hands slid up his chest and around his neck. "So damn much."

His hand moved to the back of my head, and he cradled my face as he kissed me again, continuing to give me embraces that were soft but packed with passion. His fingertips gently dug into my hair before he moved his hand under the fall of my strands.

I got lost in him immediately, my fingers gliding through his hair. I felt complete the second he returned to me. His affection was exactly what I'd been craving since the moment he walked out the door.

Now that he was back, I felt whole again.

He ended the embrace again and stared at my face, his thumb gently stroking my cheek. His eyes shifted back and forth slightly as he looked at me. He did something he'd never done before and leaned in to kiss me on the forehead. He left his kiss there, soft and warm. The heat radiated all the way down my spine and to my ass because the touch was so powerful. A man had never kissed me that way. He pulled his lips away and looked me in the eyes again. "I love you, Vanessa."

I heard every word that came out of his mouth, but it took an entire span of ten seconds to understand those words were real. They were really spoken aloud, coming from his mouth and landing on my ears. After I confirmed it was real and not a lie from my imagination, I took a deep breath because my lungs ached for oxygen. "What…?"

His thumb continued to glide across my cheek. "You heard me."

My eyes watered, the flood of tears beginning to emerge.

"I went Lake Garda and stood on the bank where you painted me. I stared at the trees, the water, the snow…and I knew."

The tears piled up at the corners of my eyes until they spilled over and streaked down my cheeks.

His thumb caught one and wiped it away. "And I know you love me too."

Shock, terror, and pain seared my entire body. I'd struggled with this relationship for the last three months because I hated my feelings for him, but this crossed a line. I didn't even know how bad things had gotten between us. "I don't love you…"

He cocked his head slightly, but his expression didn't change.

I pulled away from his grasp, getting his hands off me. "This is over." I didn't want his hands on me ever again. I never wanted the touch of my enemy, of this man who brainwashed me into thinking this relationship was okay. I'd fallen so far, but I wasn't going to fall anymore. This was a deal-breaker.

Because it was so fucked up.

I stepped farther away, putting more space in between us.

He dropped his hands, his blue eyes flashing with hostility.

"We're done." I wiped away the tear that streaked down my cheek. "Get out of my apartment."

Bones didn't move an inch. "Baby—"

"I mean it. I don't want you anywhere near me. I don't want you in my apartment ever again. I want you to just disappear. I would much rather fight you with my family then go down this road."

"Vanessa, I would never hurt your family. I'm dropping my vendetta for good."

It was something I'd never thought he would offer, and I couldn't believe he'd actually put it on the table. But I knew it was too good to be true. "For now. Then when this goes south, you'll change your—"

"No." His eyes flashed in anger. "Regardless of what happens tonight, I won't touch them. I know how much they mean to you, and I would never hurt someone you love…because I love you."

More tears emerged, angry tears. "Stop saying that. You're not the kind of man who loves anyone."

"No. I'm not the kind of man who lies. I know how I feel about you, and I'm not going to lie about it. Just because I've never loved a woman before doesn't mean I'm incapable of loving you better than any man ever could." His arms remained by his sides and he didn't move closer to me, but I felt like his body still surrounded mine. He shot me a look of hostility mixed with disappointment. "I didn't think we would end up here, and as annoyed as I am about it, I'm not going to pretend nothing happened. You think I want to be in love with my enemy's daughter? You think I want to drop this vendetta? You fucked up everything, baby.

But, you know? I'm okay with it. I'm okay with it because you're the one woman I can't stop thinking about. You're the one woman I respect. You're the one woman I want to protect. So be strong and just be real with me."

"I am being real," I said through my tears. "This is just lust, not love. This is just convenience. We've been using each other for months, and that's all it's ever been. That's all it will ever be. I'm done."

He took a deep breath, one full of frustration. His chest rose with the movement, his immense body looking bigger.

"I never should have shown you that painting…" It led to all of this. My mother came to the same conclusion when she saw it, and now Bones did the same. "You're seeing something that's not there. It's just a painting. It's just paint and canvas. You think you see the way I feel, but you don't."

"I don't need to be a professional to know what I saw. Anyone would draw the same conclusion—and you know it."

I looked away, thinking of the words my mother said. "I don't love you…"

"Say it as many times as you want. Doesn't change anything."

I lifted my gaze again. "You told me I had my rights. And I'm telling you I want you to leave and never come back. I'm telling you this is never going to happen. I'm telling you I want nothing to do with you."

I threw my hands down, disgusted with myself for letting this continue for so long. Three months of my life came and went—and I spent all of that with this man.

Bones didn't move toward the door. "Cut the bullshit."

"It's not bullshit."

"The second I walked through that door, you were all over me."

"Because I want to fuck you, not because I love you." I crossed my arms over my chest, feeling my life spin out of control. "If you won't hurt my family and I'm not a prisoner, then I want nothing to do with you. I want you to walk out and never come back. I won't change my mind."

He still didn't move. He hadn't blinked once throughout the entire conversation. He kept his anger restrained while I had my breakdown. With a clenched jaw and flared nostrils, he looked like he wanted to strangle me. "If you really want me to leave you alone, you're going to have to give me a real reason. Because I know you love me. I'm watching tears streak down your cheeks, and I still see it. So don't waste your time thinking you're fooling me. Maybe you're fooling yourself, but I know you're smarter than that."

I wiped my tears away with my fingertips and sniffed. "There's no future for us. Even if I loved you, and I'm not saying I do, it would never work. Your father killed my aunt…he raped my mother…and you kept me as a prisoner for the last three months—"

"You weren't a prisoner, and you know it."

"Whatever," I said. "It's not a fairy tale."

"A woman like you doesn't need a fairy tale. You said your family wants you to marry a powerful man." He raised up both of his arms, showing the definition of his arms. "Well, I'm the most powerful. I'm bullet-proof. And I'm rich. I'd take care of you better than your own father did."

"No…" More tears burned in my eyes. "I will never love a man who's hurt my family so much…"

"I never did anything, Vanessa. Don't hold me accountable for my father's actions."

"You wanted to kill my entire family, so I have to. What if this hadn't happened? You could be butchering my family right this very moment."

"But it didn't happen," he said quietly. "At this very moment, I'm telling you I love you. That's what's real. I said I wouldn't hurt your family. I've sacrificed my blood lust—for you. That says a lot more than my genealogy."

"My father is the most stubborn man on this planet…sometimes my mom is worse. They'll never accept us. They'll never accept you."

"I don't give a damn if they do. We're in this relationship together—not with your family."

"My family is the most important thing in the world to me… I would never be with someone they hated."

"Then don't tell them about me. Problem solved."

"You'd rather be a secret?"

"It's not like I want to spend any time with your family anyway. I said I wouldn't kill them, but that doesn't mean I'll stop hating them."

"How can you say that and still want to be with me?"

"I already said this," he snapped. "I'm with you —not them."

"My family dates who I date…and I'm not going to lie to them. I'm not going to have a secret life they don't know about. They're resourceful and smart. They'll figure it out eventually. And that's the last thing I want…for them to know I'm in love with the son of the man who hurt my family."

His eyes narrowed on my face, reacting to my choice of words.

Shit.

He didn't grin like an arrogant asshole. He was too angry for that right now. "Even if we didn't have a long-term future together, we could still be together now. We could still enjoy each other—honestly."

That was not an improvement. I couldn't get more attached to him than I already was. "No."

"Why?"

"I can't let this get any worse. I'll never marry you, so I'm setting myself up for agonizing pain. I'm just going to hurt my family. I can't stand my father's disappointment, and if he knew about this…he would never look at me the same."

"You're a grown-ass woman, Vanessa. Be with the man you want to be with. You don't need your father's blessing."

"Yes, I do," I said firmly. "I need it more than anything else in this world. My parents mean everything to me. I know you don't get that because—"

"I don't have parents?" His nostrils flared again. "Because my father was killed by your parents? Because my mother turned into a prostitute to take care of me? Because her throat was slit, and she was left in a dumpster? Yeah, I didn't have the perfect fucking childhood you had, and honestly, I hate you for it. You had everything that should have been mine. I hate you, and I hate your family too. But I can look past that since whatever the fuck we have is so damn good. Tell me it's not good. Tell me it's not the best high you've ever had."

I couldn't. It would be the most obvious lie I've ever told.

"I don't care about my parents or your parents right now. This is just between the two of us."

"But you don't get it…this can't go anywhere. I don't want to get involved if we have no future. I want to get married and have my own family, and for that to happen, I need to pick someone my family can be close with. He doesn't have to be perfect. He just can't be you…"

He clenched his jaw, his teeth grinding together. "If I can drop the vendetta when it's been my life goal, then your father should be able to drop his prejudice—"

"He never will. My father is pragmatic and logical, but this…is something he'll never accept. He'll never accept you, Bones. Your father raped and killed his sister. If that wasn't bad enough, your father raped my mother. This can't happen. Not now and not ever."

He finally turned quiet, his jaw loosened in disappointment.

"This is over…" I wouldn't love him, and I wouldn't let him love me. I had to move on with my life. I had to find someone better, someone my family could love. It wasn't Bones, and it would never be Bones. "For good."

He never severed eye contact with me, watching me with the same intensity as before. His hands relaxed, and he dropped the fists he'd been holding during the duration of the conversation.

Silence passed between, so heavy and painful.

This was the last time I would ever see him.

It hurt so much that I thought my chest would crack inward. "If you're still going to kill my family—"

"I'm not," he said quickly. "I promise."

I stared at him in disbelief.

"They're safe—because of you." He turned away from me and headed to the door, taking my words seriously. I wouldn't change my mind about this, and there was nothing he could say to make me rethink this horrid relationship. He unlocked the door and turned back to me. "I want you to do me a favor."

"Okay…"

"Move in to a better apartment. Because I won't be outside to keep you safe anymore."

I DIDN'T SLEEP at all that night.

All I could think about was Bones. The way he said those words.

I love you, Vanessa.

He sounded so sincere when he said them, looked me right in the eye as he spoke. He said he would drop the blood war for good, regardless of if I reciprocated his affection or not. The terror that kept me up at night had finally passed; my family was safe.

But that wasn't enough to get me to stay.

We had no future—plain and simple.

All we had was hot sex and lustful affection.

I had to forget him and move on with my life. I had to meet a man who was better suited for me, someone my father would like and want spend time with. I wanted someone I could bring for the holidays. With Bones, it would only ostracize me from my family. My parents would never turn their backs on me, but it would put a thick wedge between us.

My father would be so angry, angrier than I'd ever seen him. He wouldn't allow his only daughter to love the son of the man who raped his wife.

Just not possible.

We had worse odds than Romeo and Juliet.

I repeated this to myself over and over again, trying to console myself that I'd made the right decision.

The only decision, really.

But fuck, everything hurt.

My chest hurt. My eyes were puffy. Every breath I took hurt more than the previous one. My hands felt shaky. My skin was ice-cold and clammy. I felt like I'd lost a part of me when I told him to leave and not come back. He put up a fight most of the time, but once he realized I wouldn't change my mind, he finally left.

And then it was over.

Before I knew it, it was morning. Sun filtered through the window, and it was a nice day. There wasn't a cloud in the sky, so the light would be perfect for my artwork. But I didn't care about making a new piece.

The painting I made for him, the one of myself on his bed, was still in my bedroom.

He forgot to take it with him.

I wondered if he would be back for it.

I sat up in bed and ran my fingers through my hair, trying to chase away the headache that pounded behind my eyes. I should pop a few painkillers, but I lacked the motivation.

My phone started to ring.

I hoped it was him. I wanted to see his name on the screen. But I also didn't want it to be him either.

It was my mom.

I didn't want to talk to her right now, but I also needed to talk to her. There was something about my mother that I always found comforting. She was compassionate and understanding, possessing a soft side she didn't show to just anyone. She'd always been my mother when I was growing up, but once I became an adult, she became my friend.

My best friend.

I answered. "Hey, Mama…"

"Hey, sweetheart," she said with enthusiasm. "You'll never believe it. After the weather cleared up, we got a whole new horde of people at the winery. And we sold all your paintings! All of them. They sold like hot cakes."

It was a dream come true, but I couldn't bring myself to care. My paintings didn't seem important anymore, not in comparison to the pain inside my heart. I felt like someone stabbed me. No, I felt like someone shot me, and I was still in a state of shock. "That's great…"

Mom paused for a moment, digesting my tone. The sound of her moving in the background burst through the phone, like she was stepping into a different room so she could speak to me in private. "Sweetheart, what's wrong?"

"It's nothing… I just have a headache."

"Vanessa," she pressed. "Talk to me. Is it that man you're seeing?"

How did she know that? She always knew every-thing. I couldn't keep my tears back, and they immediately poured out. "Yes…" I cried into the phone, doing my best to keep everything back, but it was pointless. I sobbed to my mother, feeling like a teenager who just got her heart broken.

"Baby…what happened?"

"I broke up with him."

"Why?"

"He told me he loved me." I took a deep breath and forced my tears back, that way I could talk without drowning out my own words. "I told him I didn't feel the same way."

"But you do love him."

I didn't deny it anymore. "I don't want to love him… He's not right for me."

"In what way?"

I could never tell her the truth, regardless of how much I loved her. "I don't see a future with him. He's not the kind of man you marry. He's not… I don't know. Our relationship started as a fling, and it's been deep and intense…but that's all it is. I don't want to feel this way, I don't want to miss him, and I know I did the right thing…but it hurts."

My mom didn't react to my confession about my physical relationship with him. She knew I was an adult, had been an adult for a long time, and she never told me how to live my life. I never felt judgment from her, and I was certain she never told my father these things. "He's the first man you've ever loved?"

"Yes…" And I suspected he might be the only man I ever loved.

"Are you sure he's not right for you?"

Without a doubt. "Yes."

"I know this is a long shot, but could I meet him?"

Even if Bones would never hurt her, I didn't want her anywhere near him. "No, I don't think that's a good idea."

"Alright." My mom didn't push. "If you really know he's not the right man for you, then you made the right decision. It'll be hard, but it'll get easier in time. Just stay busy. Come down here for another visit if you want. But if you're unsure…maybe you should give it a chance."

If I told her who he really was, she would freak out —and my mother never freaked out. My father would be on a chopper in less than ten minutes, and my entire family would be moving in to rip his head off. I could never take Bones to a family dinner like everything was casual. My father would consider it treason if I brought his worst enemy into his own home. "I'm sure."

"Then I'm sorry, sweetheart. Heartache is the worst kind of pain. It takes a long time to heal. But eventually, it will. Just be patient."

"Thanks, Mama."

"Of course, sweetheart."

A WEEK WENT BY, and I didn't hear from him. I tried to stay busy like my mother recommended, so I worked on my artwork, went for long runs, went to the grocery store, and actually tried to cook.

The tracker was still in my ankle, but I didn't ask him to remove it.

I was afraid it would make a bloody mess.

And a part of me didn't mind leaving it in there.

I'd ended our relationship, but I guess I wasn't quite ready to let it go. I'd wondered if he'd found another woman by now, paid a few prostitutes to entertain him every night so he could forget about me quicker.

It made me sick to my stomach.

I should go out and start meeting new guys so my heart would heal faster, but I honestly didn't want anyone else. I didn't want to go through the process of getting to know someone, of trying to find a connection strong enough so I would have good sex. It happened sometimes, but after being with a man like Bones, I knew I would never find it again.

Everything would be mediocre in comparison.

A few days later, there was a knock on my door.

My heart leaped into my throat when I thought of Bones. Maybe he decided to stop by. Maybe he wanted to try to persuade me to change my mind.

I wanted to change my mind…but I never could.

I looked through the peephole and saw my mother on the other side.

The last person I expected.

"Mama?" I opened the door and saw her smiling in front of me. "What are you doing here?"

"Well, the weather is nice, so I thought we would go shopping. Your father is in town for work, so I decided I would have you entertain me."

I suspected this was all just an excuse to see me after my little meltdown over the phone. "That sounds great. Just let me grab my bag."

We went shopping downtown, picking up jewelry, new sweaters, and new shoes. Father paid for all of it, and then we had lunch. She never asked me about Bones or how I was doing. Instead, it seemed like she was trying to distract me. "Do you have any new paintings for me to bring home?"

"I only have two…"

"Two is better than none. I think we can raise the price a bit. I'm telling you, people loved them. The tourists loved them too because they got to have an original piece from an Italian artist."

"That's incredible."

"You're very talented, Vanessa. I've seen people stare at your paintings for several minutes. You make them feel something."

"I guess so."

She opened her wallet and took out the checks she'd collected. "They're all in your name, so cash them whenever you have time."

I looked through the pile and realized it was almost twenty thousand euros. "Wow…"

Mom grinned. "I kinda raised the prices when you left…and I'm glad I did. I knew you were worth more."

I folded them and placed them in my wallet. "Those paintings made me some serious money."

"They did," she said in agreement. "Keep it up."

"I guess I don't need you guys to pay my rent anymore."

Mom gave a wave. "Don't worry about that. You should save it to open that gallery or buy a house, something nice in the countryside. Unless you like living in the city…"

I wanted to move home. Now that Bones was gone, I didn't want to be here anymore. But my heart was still broken, so I wasn't ready to leave yet. "I'll think about it."

We finished our sandwiches and drinks, and Mom waved down the waiter to bring the check. "Alright… this is going to be a little weird."

"You want me to pay for lunch?" I asked with a laugh.

"No, of course not. I'd chop off your hand before I let that happen." She pulled her phone out of her purse and pulled up a picture. "I'll drop this if you want me to, but I thought I would ask. Your father has a good friend in the restaurant business. Apparently, he has a very handsome son…"

I knew exactly where this was going. My mother was setting me up.

"He went to university to study business, and now he owns a chain of restaurants in Milan. Your father likes him because he did all of that on his own and never took a single euro from his father. He's successful, humble, and from what I hear…very picky about who he dates. He's never introduced a woman to his family."

"He could be gay."

Mom chuckled. "From what I gather, he's definitely not gay. Anyway…" She set the phone on the table in front of me. "No pressure. If you don't like the guy or this is too weird, I'll drop it and never bring it up again."

Since we were on the topic, I lifted the phone and looked at the picture. The man had dark hair the way I did, along with brown eyes. He had a chiseled jaw the way I liked, and he was fit. He was definitely handsome…a lot more handsome than I expected. I handed the phone back. "How old is he?"

"He's a few years younger than Conway, so he's about five years older than you. That might seem like a lot, but most women prefer older men for a reason…a lot more mature and serious."

I knew my father was older than my mother, the age gap about the same.

"So…?"

"He's definitely good-looking. But I doubt a man like that is looking to be set up."

"Well, long story short, his father bought one of your paintings. His son saw it and really liked it…and that's how it came up. He's seen your picture and said you were a very beautiful woman."

"Wow…that must have been awkward for Father," I said with a laugh.

She shrugged. "He's not oblivious to your appearance, sweetheart. He knows he has a beautiful daughter. And he also knows you're at the age where you're looking for someone to spend your life with. At least he likes this guy."

"What's his name?

"Matteo Rossi."

The only man I wanted to be with was the one person I couldn't have…and shouldn't want to have. It was too soon to go on a date, but I didn't know what else to do. I had to move on, and the sooner I did that, the easier this would be. Knowing Bones, he'd probably already started the progress. "He's a good guy?" I wanted someone clean, someone who didn't break the law or kill people.

"Of course. Perfect gentleman. The strong and silent type. And you know he won't pull any stunts because he wouldn't cross your father. I don't think he would even go through with this unless he was genuinely interested in you."

I'd ended things with Bones because my father would never accept him. I wanted someone my family would embrace, someone they would love like family. Meeting a handsome man my father approved of seemed like the best way to accomplish that. "I'll give it a shot. Can't hurt, right?"

Mom smiled. "Nope. Can't hurt."

MY MOTHER LEFT, and I returned to the solitude of my apartment.

She cheered me up during the day, taking me shopping for cute things I didn't really need. I handed over my few new paintings for her to sell at the winery. The only one that remained behind was the painting that wasn't for sale.

It would never be for sale.

Now it hung on my bedroom wall, across from the bed. When the bedside lamp was on, I could see it well enough to study the picture, to remember the night we met with perfect clarity.

I couldn't believe I was going on a date my parents arranged.

Well, I doubted my father had much to do with it.

My mother was the mastermind behind it all.

But Matteo was handsome and successful. That was hard to find in a man, so I thought I would give it a try. If there was no connection, at least we could be friends. I doubted I would want anything romantic with him right away since Bones was heavy on my mind.

He was always on my mind.

Someone knocked on the door.

It was almost eight in the evening, far too late for someone just to drop by. There was only one person it could be, and if it wasn't him, then that would be even worse.

I looked through the peephole and lost my breath. It was him.

Enormous, powerful, and handsome, it was him.

I pressed my forehead against the door and closed my eyes, my heart beating so fast. My hand shook as I held the doorknob. He never knocked, just walked inside like he owned the place. He was respecting my space, which must be difficult for him to do.

He must have heard me on the other side of the door because he said, "Let me in, or I'll let myself in." He was hostile and aggressive. Our distance hadn't changed his character at all.

I unlocked the door and opened it.

In a black hoodie and dark jeans, he was as hand-some as ever. His blue eyes were brighter with emotion, and the lines of his jaw were more pronounced because his teeth were clenched together. He took a deep breath when he looked at me, his chest rising noticeably as the air entered his lungs. He stared at me like he loved me and hated me at the same time.

I could barely stand there and keep my distance. My hands wanted to reach for him, to grab those powerful shoulders and pull him into me. Not only did I want to kiss him, but I also just wanted to hold him. I wanted to feel those thick biceps, feel that soft mouth against mine. I wanted to wrap my ankles around his waist and keep him pressed against me. His presence reverberated inside my apartment, and I could feel it seep into my pores. I could feel my breath become shaky because the chemistry between us was still scorching.

As if nothing had happened, I wanted him all over again. As if I hadn't already made my beliefs clear, I wanted to take him to bed and ask him never to leave. My emotional response to him was more aggressive than it was before.

I forced myself to stand back, as if the distance would make this heat more bearable. "Yes?"

"I'm here for my painting."

I knew he would come for it. I'd made it just for him, and I had no use for it. I couldn't put such a provocative picture on my wall. "It's in my bedroom... I'll go get it for you." I needed an excuse to get away from him, to make sure there was as much distance between us as possible. I turned my back to him, but I could still feel his heat drill through my skin.

I walked into my bedroom, where it was wrapped up and leaning against the wall.

He followed me, his heavy footfalls hitting the floor.

I picked up the painting and turned toward him.

He was staring at the painting on the wall. He looked at it for nearly thirty seconds before he turned back to me. Fierce, his blue eyes were penetrating. He seemed annoyed by the mounted picture rather than touched. He grabbed the painting from my hands and held it with a single hand despite the weight.

We stared at each other, the heat rising.

His eyes narrowed with more anger before he

turned away and carried the painting out of my bedroom.

I followed him into the living room, watching his powerful back ripple and shift underneath his hoodie.

He walked out the door and slammed it behind him.

I couldn't believe he'd walked out without saying more than a few words to me.

I followed him outside and watched him walk down the steps. "That's all you're going to say to me?"

He stopped at the bottom and turned around to look up at me. "We had an entire conversation in there. I could hear it, and so could you." Cold like ice crystals, his blue eyes bored into mine. "You stood in that room with me and fought against what we both felt. You still want me to disappear, then fine. But you have to let me go. You can't chase me out here like I owe you something. I made a sacrifice for you, but you aren't willing to make the same sacrifice for me. So be it." He turned around again.

"You're asking me to sacrifice my family."

He turned back around. "And I already sacrificed mine." His shoulders tensed as he stared me down. "I dropped my vendetta for this. For us. For you. I committed to this with everything I had, but you turned your back." He stepped backward, still looking at me with his fierce gaze. "Now I'm turning my back on you." He turned around and walked away, his powerful physique disappearing into the darkness.

Thank you!

Thank you so much for reading Fantasy in Lingerie. I hope you enjoyed Vanessa and Bones. If so, please consider leaving a review on the site you purchased this book. It's the best way to let me know how much you enjoyed it.

Hugs,
Penelope

Also by Penelope Sky

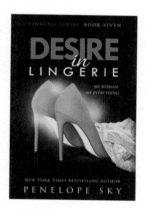

Bones is a man I despise.

He gives Bad Blood a whole new definition.

But he's not exactly what I thought he was.

Maybe men can change.

But it doesn't matter how I feel about him.

My father would never approve.

He'd never let me love a man like him.

Order Now

Made in the USA
Thornton, CO
08/16/24 10:49:00